SHELLED BY AN UNSEEN FOE

JAMES FISKE

Shelled by an Unseen Foe

James Fiske

© 1st World Library, 2009
PO Box 2211
Fairfield, IA 52556
www.1stworldlibrary.com
First Edition

LCCN: 2009923467

Softcover ISBN: 978-1-4218-8855-2
Hardcover ISBN: 978-1-4218-8954-2
eBook ISBN: 978-1-4218-8756-2

Purchase *"Shelled by an Unseen Foe"*
as a traditional bound book at:
www.1stWorldLibrary.com/purchase.asp?ISBN=978-1-4218-8855-2

1st World Library is a literary, educational organization
dedicated to:

- Creating a free internet library of downloadable ebooks

- Hosting writing competitions and offering book publishing
scholarships.

Interested in more 1st World Library books? contact:
literacy@1stworldlibrary.com
Check us out at: www.1stworldlibrary.com

1st World Library Literary Society

Giving Back to the World

"If you want to work on the core problem, it's early school literacy."

- James Barksdale, former CEO of Netscape

"No skill is more crucial to the future of a child, or to a democratic and prosperous society, than literacy."

- Los Angeles Times

"Literacy... means far more than learning how to read and write... The aim is to transmit... knowledge and promote social participation."

- UNESCO

"Literacy is not a luxury, it is a right and a responsibility. If our world is to meet the challenges of the twenty-first century we must harness the energy and creativity of all our citizens."

- President Bill Clinton

"Parents should be encouraged to read to their children, and teachers should be equipped with all available techniques for teaching literacy, so the varying needs and capacities of individual kids can be taken into account."

- Hugh Mackay

CONTENTS

CHAPTER I

THE CALL OF HOME

Reveille was over at the military school, and the three boys on the end of the line nearest the mess hall walked slowly toward the broad steps of the big brick building ahead. They differed greatly in type, but of this they were unconscious, for all were deep in thought.

"I am going home," said the tallest boy abruptly. "Had a letter from my sister last night. My word, they are having some ripping times over there!"

"Your father won't let you," said the second lad. "How can *you* go to England when *I* can't get back to Mexico?"

"I can jolly well go," said the tall boy. "I've been planning for this. Mid-term is over, and I haven't told you chaps, but I've been hoarding every cent of my allowance all winter. I have enough and to spare for second cabin."

"But your father wants you here out of harm's way," urged the Mexican.

"He *thinks* he does," said Nickell-Wheelerson smiling, his blue eyes flashing. "He *thinks* he does, but I know he is just trying me out. Here's the way it is. Dad's in the field and my second brother; you know my oldest brother was shot in the trenches in France two months ago. I'm nineteen. There are two little chaps to carry on the name and take care of the title, if the rest of us go. I've just *got* to get over there! Don't you see how it is?"

"Of course!" said the Mexican, his dark eyes glowing gloomily. "Of course you feel you've got to go! And here I must stay. I want to go home too."

"It's different with you," said Nickell-Wheelerson, patting his companion on the back. "You keep out of that mess! Mexico is going to need you worse later on."

"How about you?" demanded Morales, the Mexican. "I should think England would need you when that mess, as you call it, is finished."

"She needs me now, and I know it, and dad knows it," Nick assured him. "I'm going *home*! You'd better be glad you are not mixed up in this thing," he said, turning to the third boy. "You are safe awhile yet, you old Greece-spot, you!"

"There are some Greeks fighting; a few on the European border of the Dardanelles," said the boy addressed.

"Oh, of course you will get into it sooner or later," said Nick, "but I'm banking on that queen of yours to stall things along as far as she can. She can't put it off forever, though. You will be in it."

"As sure as my name is Zaidos," said the young Greek, "you are quite right! We will have to fight sooner or later."

"Well, don't cross bridges," said Nick. "Sit tight, and I'll go over there and help clean up things."

Light-heartedly they raced up the steep hill leading from the parade ground to the mess hall.

A slim young orderly came out of the Adjutant's office onto the terrace and looked about. Seeing the three boys, he called in a high, clear voice, "Oh, you Nosey!" and as the Greek approached added formally, "Corporal Zaidos is wanted by the Adjutant."

"What's he going to get ragged for now, I wonder," mused Nickell-Wheelerson as he and Morales joined the crowd and went into the mess hall.

Zaidos did not come back. Nick watched the door anxiously. They were room-mates, and Nick was well aware of Nosey's tendencies in the way of breaking minor rules. As soon as he could get out of the mess, he hurried down past the Adjutant's office, and hastily framing an errand, went in. The room was empty.

Nick hurried over to the barracks to their room. Sitting on the side of his narrow bunk, his hands clenched, his face white, was Zaidos.

"What's the row, old top?" Nick sang out cheerfully as he made a great pretense of picking up his books and stuffing a couple of pencils in the top of his pigskin puttee.

The young Greek shook his head, and Nick realized that it was something indeed very serious with him.

"What *is* the row, old man?" he said again, coming over and sitting beside his friend. "What has the Adjutant got in for you this time?"

"Nothing," said Zaidos. "He had a cablegram from home. It is pretty bad, Nick . . ." He paused. "My father is sick; fact is, he is dying; and I've got to leave to-night."

"Gosh!" exclaimed Nick. "That's too bad! I'm more than sorry!"

"Yes, it's bad," said Zaidos. "And the queer thing is that I don't seem to feel as sorry about my father dying as I do to think that I don't *know* him any better. Think of it, Nick, I came over here to school when I was not quite seven. My mother died when I was six, and since that I have seen my father twice; once when he came over here, and the year I went home. And it is not as though there was not plenty of money. I suppose my father is the richest man, or one of the richest men, in Greece. He's just—Oh, I don't know! He never seemed to be like a lot of fathers I have seen. I never could get *next* to him. And I've been pretty lonely most all my life. I have always planned to go back as soon as I finished school, and get acquainted with my father. I thought if I tried, I could make him like me. I suppose he does well enough, but I wanted to be chummy with him. I thought I could if I tried."

"You bet you could, Nosey!" said Nick, an arm over the bowed shoulder beside him. "You could warm up a wooden Indian, you old live-wire, you! I jolly well know you! You would get under the crust if anyone could! Perhaps it isn't as bad as they think. You go home, and perhaps your father will get better, and you will get to be the best chums in the world. Cheer up, old chap! It will come out all right. Do you really go tonight?"

"Yes, I go to-night. They have got my tickets, and now they are telephoning for my passage."

James Fiske

Nickell-Wheelerson sat thinking hard. Then he rose and bolted for the door.

"Wait!" called Zaidos. "I want you to help me pack, Nick."

But the big English boy had disappeared. In half an hour he returned, looking triumphant. He flung his trim military jacket on the bunk.

"That's done for!" he cried. He jerked a trunk into the middle of the floor and, opening it, commenced to turn out its cluttered contents.

"Come on, Nosey!" he cried. "As our American brothers put it, 'get a move on!' We have about half a day to get packed."

"Are you crazy?" demanded the Greek, staring at him.

"Not crazy, Nosey, dear chappie! Not crazy; merely going home!"

"Home?" repeated Zaidos feebly. "*Home?*"

"Home!" said Nick jubilantly. "With you! At least on the same steamer. So if they blow us up on the way over, we can soar hand in hand, old chum!"

"Well, when you get through raving, I wish you would tell how you did it."

"I simply reminded the Adjutant that the arrangement was that I was remaining here at my own discretion, as per Pater's written agreement. I said I had decided to go with you, although I had been thinking for a week that I might leave at any time. They mentioned money, and I showed my little roll. There is plenty. So I am going to-night with you. They have telephoned about a stateroom. That's all! I'm going to give all my stuff away. I won't come back."

Nickell-Wheelerson never did come back. But that is another story.

There were a lot of poor marks made that afternoon. With the two most popular fellows in the school going off, there couldn't be much studying. Everybody tried to help, and everybody got in the way and had to be stepped over or pushed over. But time passed, and good-byes were said, and the night on the swift train passed, too; and when they looked back, the following day in New York was a hurried whirl. And then they smelt the unchanging smell of the docks; sea salt and paint and tar.

They watched the last person down the gang-plank, a weeping woman it was. Then they shouted farewell to the kindly shores, and the steadfast Lady of Liberty on Governor's Island. She seemed to salute the passing ship with her uplifted torch, and the boys felt that peace and safety and prosperity lay behind them.

Then some nights and days went swiftly by, and one morning the boys clasped hands and gruffly spoke their farewells. Nickell-Wheelerson went home to find that his older brother slept in a lowly grave somewhere in France. His father, dead of his wounds, lay in the castle hall, and the boy Nick answered wearily when sorrowing footmen called him "My Lord."

But that is really the beginning of the other story.

Zaidos hurried on his way alone, and one bright morning, after many adventures, stood once more in Saloniki.

A porter came up to him, and at the same moment a man in the livery of his father's house approached and saluted him. "Your father urges you to hasten, Excellency," he said.

"Is my father very ill?" asked Zaidos.

"Very ill indeed, sir," said the man.

They started through the station and as they left the building a man approached. He spoke to Zaidos, but the boy, having spent years of his life in America, failed to catch the rapidly spoken words.

He turned to the house-servant, who stood with bulging eyes.

"What does he say?" he asked.

The man was speaking violently, then beseechingly, to the stranger, who was in uniform.

"What is it?" again demanded Zaidos. He began to get the run of the conversation, but as he made it out, it was too preposterous to consider. The officer laid a hand on his shoulder and shook his head.

"You will *have* to come," he said. "YOU ARE WANTED FOR THE ARMY."

"But my father?" said Zaidos, alarmed.

The man shrugged his shoulders. "He will die the same whether you come or not. Come!"

A grim look came into the boy's face. It alarmed the servant.

"Go, go, master," he begged. "You do not know. They take

everyone. What is to be must be. Go, I entreat you, without violence. I do not want to go and tell your father that I have seen you slain before my eyes. I will tell him you are here, and that you will come later." He drew back and bowed to the officer, who kept a hand on Zaidos' shoulder.

"Yes, tell him I will come soon," said Zaidos. "Go to him quickly."

The man turned and hurried away.

"Give up all thought of going," said the officer. "It is a pity —one owes a great duty to one's father; but we need you now. And the need of country comes first."

"But Greece is not in the war!" said Zaidos as they hurried along the street.

"No, not yet; but there are places enough to guard, so we need more men than we dreamed. But I talk too much. Here is the headquarters. Let me advise you not to bother the Colonel with demands to visit your home."

They entered the big, dingy room of the police station which had been transformed into a sort of recruiting station. The officer in charge was an overbearing First Lieutenant who was overworked, tired and irritable. He had come from a distant part of Greece, and the name of Zaidos carried no weight with him. He shook his head when Zaidos made his request. He even smiled a little. "Too thin, too thin!" he said. "I should say that all the mothers and fathers, and most of the uncles and aunts and cousins in the world are ill," he sneered. "No, you can't go. Get back there in line and wait for your squad to be outfitted."

Zaidos shrugged his shoulders and obeyed, well knowing

that, once in uniform, even that display of feeling would be absolutely out of order. He had been too long in a military school to misunderstand military procedure, and he knew that whatever queer chance had placed him in his present position, the thing was done now. He was to see real fighting.

Zaidos had a lion's heart and was absolutely ignorant of fear, but he worried when he thought of the possible effect on his father. He, poor man, would feel that his natural wish to behold his only son once more had placed the boy in a position of the gravest danger; indeed, in the path of almost certain death. What the effect of this knowledge would be on his health, Zaidos trembled to consider. But he was powerless to avoid the shock to his father, and once more shrugging his shoulders he stepped into line.

After a tedious delay, during which the men and boys who were unaccustomed to any sort of drill shifted uneasily from foot to foot, shuffled, twisted, and fretted generally, while Zaidos alone stood easily at attention, the order was given for the squad to go into another room.

Here they were registered, examined physically, and equipped with uniforms. Then they were finally taken to the mess hall and provided with a wholesome, plain meal which they proceeded to enjoy to the utmost. Zaidos could not eat. He toyed with the food, his quick brain ever planning some way by which he could get to his father. The more he thought of it the more it seemed to be his duty to do so at *any* cost. But he seemed surrounded by barriers. He could not see a way clear. So he resigned himself for the present, and marched to the dormitory where his squad was quartered. It had been a trying and exhausting day for everyone and his peasant companions, accustomed to bed-time at sunset, soon threw themselves down and slept.

The sleeping quarters were on the ground floor. Zaidos found his pallet behind a great door opening on the street. It was open a trifle, but a heavy chain secured it from opening any further. Zaidos stuck his head out. There was enough space for that. It was the blackest night he had ever seen, if one could be said to see anything as dark.

A sentry padded up and down in the blackness. Zaidos smiled. The man could certainly not see five feet ahead of him. All the city lights were out for safety's sake. As he approached, Zaidos drew back, and lay staring at the ceiling.

A stifled sob startled him. He turned. On the next pallet a young fellow lay face downward, and muffled his weeping in the coarse blanket. For an hour Zaidos listened. The shaken breathing and occasional sobs continued. Zaidos could stand it no longer. He reached over and let a friendly clasp fall on the heaving shoulder.

"What is it?" he whispered in his best Greek.

The young fellow turned to him eagerly, glad of sympathy. In a rush of words that made it hard for Zaidos to understand, he whispered his story. There was a wife and a little, little baby, "Oh, *so* little!" far up on the mountain-side; they would starve; surely, *surely* they would starve! They did not know what had become of him. Zaidos tried in vain to calm the man. He could not do so and finally dropped into a restless sleep with the man's stifled sobs ringing in his ears.

Zaidos had to concede that the man's fate was a hard one. He was only nineteen years of age. The girl-wife was seventeen. As Zaidos dropped asleep he was reflecting that no doubt nine-tenths of the men sleeping in that room carried burdens as well as the young mountaineer and himself.

James Fiske

He was wakened awhile later by a touch on the shoulder nearest the door. A voice addressed him. For a moment Zaidos was unable to locate it. Then he discovered that it was coming from the partly open door. It was the young husband who had sobbed in the dark.

"Waken, friend!" said the low whisper. "Waken! Farewell! I go! There is a small packet under my pallet. I forgot it. Will you hand it quickly before the sentry turns?"

"Don't do a fool stunt like that," said Zaidos in English.

The deserter repeated, "Quickly, quickly!" and as Zaidos handed him the packet he disappeared, the night swallowing him in its blackness. Zaidos crawled to the door and, flat on the floor, put his head out the opening into the street. All was quiet. The sentry marched up and down the long block with the dragging slowness of a weary man. The mountaineer had escaped!

Somewhere a clock struck eleven booming strokes. Zaidos could not believe that it was so early, but immediately another faint chime verified the first. Here and there in the room heavy snoring or muttered words sounded. There were no guards in the room as the door was locked.

Eleven o'clock! Five hours before daylight. A daring thought flashed into Zaidos' head. He knelt and once more leaned through the opening of the door. He thanked his schoolboy leanness. There *was* enough space! He waited until the sentry's heavy footfall dragged to the end of the block; then with a struggle he twisted through the door and stood in the open, deserted street.

In the years of his absence he had forgotten the city, but he remembered the general directions, and only yesterday he had seen in the distance the gleaming white marble walls of his home standing on the beautiful headland overlooking the blue waters of the bay. He heard the sentry approaching and, trusting to instinct, turned into the nearest street and hurried away.

It seemed to Zaidos that the journey was endless, yet he went like the wind. He found himself searching the east for dawn. His instinct did for him what sight and reason would have failed to do. In daylight he would have been lost, but in that black darkness he kept his course, and finally the great white building where his fathers for generations had lived loomed mysteriously before him. He hurried up the broad stairs and besieged the massive doors with heavy blows. A startled footman opened it, and with a curt word Zaidos entered and demanded his father. The man bowed and led him up to a closed door. Here he knocked softly and a stout old woman answered. She looked hard at the young man in uniform, then with a little cry clasped him in a warm embrace. It was his old nurse.

"Ah," she cried, "God has answered my prayers! You are in time!"

A chill of apprehension swept over the boy. "Is he so ill?" he asked.

"He has waited for you," she answered. "I told him you would come. I knew it. He has been dying for many days, but he would not go until he saw you."

"Let me come," said Zaidos. He dashed past the old woman, the nurses and the doctors, and was clasped in his father's arms.

CHAPTER II

AN IMPRESSED SOLDIER

The events of that night long remained in Zaidos' memory, a blurred picture of pain and heart-break. There was a brief and precious hour with the father whom he had so seldom seen; a time filled with the priceless last communications which seemed to bridge all absence and bring them close, close together at last. His coming seemed to fill his dying father with a strange new strength. He talked rationally and earnestly with his beloved son. Zaidos could not believe that the end was near. Count Zaidos gave the boy a paper containing a list of the places where the family treasure was put away or concealed. Also other papers of the greatest value. Without these he would be unable to prove his heirship to the title and estates of the Zaidos family. In case of the boy's death all would go to a distant cousin, Velo Kupenol, who had long made his home with the Count. Zaidos turned to meet this cousin, whom he had not seen for so many years that his existence had been forgotten. He saw a keen, ferret-faced lad, a little older than himself. He took an instant dislike to the boy, and rebuked himself for doing so. Yet the hard eyes looked *too* steadily into his, with a cold, piercing, deadly look.

"I'm in the way," thought Zaidos, as he turned again to his

father. And some sure instinct in his heart cried, "Beware, beware!"

When the dying Count handed the thin packet of precious papers to his son, Zaidos slipped them in the inner pocket of his blouse. At that moment Velo approached the bedside.

"Uncle," he said, "unfortunately my cousin here has been impressed into service. Would it not be well for *me* to keep these papers? I would guard them with my life, and as I do not intend to fight they would be safe with me in any case."

The Count frowned. "No," he cried. "Velo Kupenol, I have not found you true to your name! You have been here with me for years, and I know you through and through. I have treated you with all patience, have paid your debts, have saved you from disgrace for the sake of the family. I have forgiven you over and over. You have not shown me even the loyalty that a true friend would expect, to say nothing of a relative. If anything happens to my son, unfortunately the estates will be yours; but while he lives, the papers will remain in *his* possession, to do with as he sees fit. Ah!" he cried, turning to his son, "be worthy of our name, my boy! No Zaidos has ever yet disgraced it. I put my trust in you, and I know you will not fail me. To the day she died, your mother planned great things for her baby boy. She—"

He fixed his eyes on space. A look of surprise and happiness lit his face. Slowly he raised his arms as though in greeting, then sank back, dead.

Zaidos, kneeling, buried his face in the pillow. So it was over, all over! Someone raised him to his feet, as the nurse tenderly drew the sheet over his father's face. He lifted it and with one last lingering look replaced it gently, then left the room.

James Fiske

The clock struck three.

As he sank wearily in a chair, the old nurse entered. Her face was stained with tears. She glanced about, then seized Zaidos by the arm.

"*Don't trust Velo!*" she whispered, and left his side. None too soon, for Velo entered the room and with a gesture dismissed the old servant.

"Now, Zaidos," he said abruptly, "we will talk. You are *crazy* to carry such valuables around with you. After we have had breakfast, we will decide where to keep those papers. I am the next in line, as you know, and it is only just that I should know where they are in case you should get in trouble."

Zaidos shook his head. "I shall keep the papers," he said. "Of course you may remain here. I shall always look out for you. I shall not be killed in this fighting; I feel it."

"So have other men," sneered Velo. "How did you get away?"

Zaidos told him.

"Do you mean that you could not get permission, and that you escaped and came anyhow?" he asked, an evil gleam lighting his narrow eyes.

"That's about it," said Zaidos, nodding. "I must go back at once. The doctor's car will take me close to the barracks. I must get there before dawn." He went to the window and looked out. "I have no time to waste!" he cried.

"But look here, if you are caught, it means desertion,"

said Velo.

"Yes!"

"In war-time that means death," said Velo.

"Yes, but I am not going to be caught," answered Zaidos.

"Then you must hurry," declared his cousin. "Wait here just a moment, and I will see that the car is ready and get a cloak to cover you. I almost fear you have waited too long, cousin," and hurried, from the room with a last sidelong look at Zaidos' bent head.

Five minutes passed; then with a last look at his father's closed door, Zaidos went down and found Velo standing beside the automobile, talking to the chauffeur. Already the intense blackness of the night was lifting. Zaidos felt a chill of apprehension.

"You will have to hurry," said his cousin. "I will come down later and look you up. Hope you get back." He stepped back, and the car shot forward, but only for a short distance. With a queer grinding noise the engine stopped. The driver leaped out and examined it with a flashlight. He uttered an exclamation of dismay.

"Someone has put sand in the engine!" he exclaimed. "Yet I have been in it all night long!"

"You *must* have left it," said Zaidos. "Or did you go to sleep?"

"Yes, yes!" stammered the driver excitedly. "I was called away just now, when Velo Kupenol sent me to my master to tell him that I was to take you back to barracks. Ah, what shall we do?"

"How far is it?" demanded Zaidos. The night was lifting. He shivered.

"A mile straight down that avenue, Excellency, until you reach the great fountain in the public square. Then a half block to the left. You cannot miss it, but you cannot make it before dawn."

"Good-bye!" called Zaidos. He started down the wide avenue with the gentle, easy stride that had made him the best long-distance runner in school. His wind was perfect and he covered ground like a deer; but clearer and clearer as he raced he could see the grey forms of surrounding objects take shape. He reached the fountain in the public square; he made the turn to the left and slowed to a walk. The sentry, walking slowly, reached the opposite corner, and before Zaidos could reach the open door he turned. It was too late to turn back. Zaidos squared his shoulders and approached. The sentry eyed him sharply and was about to speak but Zaidos said, "Good-morning," with civil ease. The man returned the salutation. Then, "What are you doing here?" he questioned.

"With a letter," said Zaidos, tapping his pocket.

"Where from?" demanded the sentry.

"Over there," said Zaidos, nodding his head in the direction of the avenue. It was a bold shot, but it carried.

"Oh!" said the sentry. "The other barracks, eh? Well, will your errand wait, or must I wake them up within?"

"There is no hurry at all," said Zaidos, easily. "I must see the commanding officer by seven o'clock, that's all."

"Very well," said the man. "I'll take you in then. I'm tired enough myself tramping up and down here all night. That place is full of recruits, and a lot of them are unwilling ones, I can tell you. But they are under lock and key. They can't escape. All the air they get even is from that crack in the door. A fly couldn't get out there." He was a fat sentry, and he laughed. Zaidos joined his mirth.

"Perhaps a thin fly might," he said.

The man shrugged. "Perhaps!" he said. "Those recruits are raw, I can tell you. You can be glad you are a trained soldier. I could tell it by your walk, even in this dim light. The walk always tells."

Zaidos nodded and squatted down near the open door. Moment by moment his danger was growing. The sentry turned and sauntered to the end of the block. Zaidos counted slowly. Once the man turned and nodded in a friendly fashion, then resumed his slow pace. Sixty steps. He stood for a moment on the corner, then came back. "Not long now," he said, and smiled. Then he passed in the other direction. Eighty steps that way. Zaidos counted. Again the man returned. Zaidos could feel his muscles stiffening, as if about to spring. He cautiously shifted to a position still nearer the partly open door and measured the opening. He felt heavy and awkward. He studied the dark opening. It did indeed look very narrow. He had squirmed through it without much trouble, but that was in the densest darkness, and he had taken all the time he needed. Now if the sentry should turn * * * Well, it would be the end of Zaidos, and a most ignominious end at that. He was not a coward, but he had no fancy to find himself against a wall with a firing squad before him.

Sixty steps and back walked the sentry, and Zaidos, head

against the wall, body reclining close to the open door, seemed to be dozing. One, two, three steps past him, went the sentry again—

With the quickness of a cat Zaidos ripped off his uniform blouse, thrust it through the door, stretched his arms over his head, and with a mighty shove of his strong young legs thrust himself into the opening.

There was a terrific struggle for a moment, a series of agile twists, and Zaidos fell forward on the stone floor. Quickly he kicked away his shoes and tumbled down on his pallet. After the gray dawn outside the room was very dark. He heard the sentry outside come running to the door, push it against its stout chain and stand thinking. Zaidos laughed to himself. The opening, "too small for a fly," had swallowed him; and the unsuspicious fellow outside was filled with almost superstitious amazement. He knew that Zaidos could not by any possibility have reached the corner without making the least sound, and the street was absolutely silent. Zaidos, scarcely daring to breathe, smiled in the dark.

Then, fatherless and friendless as he was, and thrust by a strange fate of birth into a war in which he had no part, Zaidos, exhausted by his night's experiences, dropped asleep. About him men tired by a long night spent on pallets as hard as the stone flooring tossed and groaned or sighed wakefully. Zaidos slept on.

He was sleeping so heavily an hour later that he did not hear two soldiers enter with a slender young fellow in civilian dress. He never stirred as they went from pallet to pallet, scanning the faces as they passed. When they reached his side the young man looked down at him with an expression which might have been taken for startled amazement if anyone had been watching. He nodded to the officers, and spoke a word of thanks. "This is my cousin," he said in a low voice. "With your permission I will sit here by him until he awakes. It would be cruel to rouse him only to tell him of his father's death."

"Yes, you may stay," said the older soldier. "There can be no objection to that."

They turned and soon the distant door closed behind them. Then the newcomer did a strange thing. He cast a swift glance over the sleeping faces, to assure himself that he was not watched, and with the light-fingered stealth of the born thief, he slipped his thin hand into Zaidos' breast pocket. Withdrawing it, he smiled wickedly at the sight of what he held. He rose to his feet, hastily pocketed his find, and for a moment stood looking down at Zaidos. With a noiseless laugh he nodded sneeringly at the sleeping boy, picked his way carefully among the men and left the room.

When Velo Kupenol had sifted sand in the engine of the automobile, he had made his first move in a dastardly campaign. Most of his life had been spent surrounded by the ease and luxury of the Zaidos castle. He had had horses and automobiles to use; he had had great stretches of park and woodland to roam through and hunt over. And best of all, he had had the best teachers in all Greece. But these he had neglected and defied at every possible turn. Velo Kupenol was lazy, cowardly and deceitful. That he was not yet a criminal was due to the watchful care and great forgiveness of the uncle who had befriended him. In the past few years this forgiveness had been stretched to its utmost. Velo himself was not aware of the number of disgraceful things his uncle had had to face for his sake. But it would have mattered not at all. He did not know the meaning of gratitude. This boy, who should have been on his knees beside the death-bed of the truest friend of his life, shedding the tears that are an honor to true men, had instantly, with his uncle's last breath, bent his quick and wicked brain on the problem of wresting the Zaidos title and estates from his cousin. The knowledge that the kindness and forbearance of the father would be continued on the part of the son never occurred to him. He would have laughed if it had. It was all or nothing. He determined that the cruel chance of war was on his side. So he dropped sand in the engine when he had sent the chauffeur on an errand, and then had hurried to headquarters. And it happened that while Zaidos sat on the sidewalk beside the chained door, talking to the friendly sentry, Velo himself was at the *front* door of the barracks waiting for it to be opened for visitors.

Fortunately, in telling Velo of his escape from barracks, Zaidos did not go into details, so Velo did not know of the door through which Zaidos had crept. He had taken it for granted that he had slipped unnoticed through the door at which he himself was standing, and as he waited he momentarily expected his cousin to come hurrying up. Velo smiled. He hoped Zaidos would come. He wanted to be there when he tried to make his lame excuses for leaving the barracks in the face of the refusal to give him permission. Velo knew well that in the troubled times in which Greece found herself, no excuse would be accepted. It was desertion; and the fact of his return would not soften the offense. There was no place or time for punishment or imprisonment. Velo shuddered, but smiled evilly.

However, Zaidos did not appear, time passed, and finally the doors opened. Velo, very humble and apologetic, made his simple request that he should be allowed to speak with his cousin who was with the soldiers in the inner room. The request was granted, and with two soldiers he entered the room full of sleeping men. He went from cot to cot, making an idle examination of each face. He was waiting for the moment when he could turn to his escort and say, "He is not here."

But there he was! Velo could not believe his senses. The soldiers, seeing that he had found his relative, turned back to the door, and Velo noiselessly knelt beside the sleeper. He stared long and curiously at the serene and open face. How he had returned was a mystery which maddened him. He was foiled for the present at least; but securing the coveted papers, he silently withdrew.

"Did you find him?" asked the young officer in charge, as Velo came up to his desk.

"Yes, thank you," said Velo, "but he could not tell me what I wanted to know. I wanted tidings of a cousin, the son of Count Zaidos, who died last night."

"Zaidos?" said the officer. "That's the name of one of our recruits."

"Yes, he is my cousin," said Velo. "But not the one we want. This fellow in here is a lazy no-account, and the army is the best place for him, although I am sorry to say so."

"Yes, the army nowadays is a good place for lazy-bones," agreed the officer. A queer look came over his face. "We are picking up all the single men we can." He leaned on the desk and spoke as one man to another. "You see we found that the army had to be doubled in short order and the only way to do it was to insist on compulsory enlistment. That's the reason," he continued calmly, "that you are now a private in the army of Greece."

"Me? Oh, no!" said Velo hastily. "It is impossible. I—I— have other things to consider. You will have to excuse me, Captain."

"I am Lieutenant," said the officer, "but you will learn the difference in rank shortly."

"But I can't *do* it!" said Velo violently, a red flush mounting to his forehead. "I simply *can't* do it! Why, my uncle died last night, and unless we find his son I am the only heir. I have *got* to stay here. I am the heir doubtless."

"That's fine!" said the officer, smiling. "In case you are shot, which is likely, all your property will revert to the crown. Greece is going to need all she can raise. I hope your uncle is rich."

Velo could not keep from boasting.

"One of the richest men in the country!" he bragged.

"Fine, fine!" said the officer. Then his manner changed. "Now, my boy, your name and address. This is straight. We need you."

Velo mumbled his name, a deadly fear growing in him. He was a coward and the thought of bloodshed filled him with a cold, deadly terror.

He regarded the Lieutenant with staring eyes. His teeth chattered.

The young officer smiled. He called two soldiers.

"Take this man to the South Barracks," he said coldly. "Under guard," he added significantly. He knew men. He saw that the boy before him would have to be whipped into shape. He thought of a recruit made the day before. Zaidos his name was. He remembered with respect and appreciation the manner of the lad. He looked once more at the new recruit. Then he took a piece of paper from his desk, wrote one word on it, addressed it "Officer in Command at South Recruiting Station," handed it to one of the soldiers standing beside Velo, and turned away. For him the incident was closed.

But Velo, feeling as though he was under arrest, walked miserably and fearfully through the streets, a soldier on either side, wondering with all his might what was written in the folded paper.

He finally asked the bearer to let him see it, but the soldier refused scornfully. As they neared the South Station his fears grew, if such a thing could be possible. Once more he tried to get the mysterious note. He had some money with him. He tried to bribe the man. For answer the soldier struck him in the face. Velo sunk into a sulky silence, and stood with eyes on the ground while the officer in charge opened the message and read the single word therein.

"Good enough!" he exclaimed. "Just what we need!" and waved the two men toward an inner room where Velo was stripped of his comfortable clothes and fitted to the new uniform of the Greek Army.

And not until then did he find out his fate. A third man sauntered up and stood watching.

"Rank and file?" he said jestingly.

"No," said the man who had carried the note. "Stoker!"

Velo thought his heart would break.

CHAPTER III

ONLY A STOKER

Zaidos was the last person in the room to awaken. Half a dozen of the groups nearest the door had filed out, answered roll call, and stood at attention in the street when a man shook him roughly by the shoulder and roused him.

"Get up, lazy-bones," he cried gruffly, "else you will feel the flat of a sword! Here you have been snoring since early last evening. How can there be so much sleep in thee, I wonder? One would nearly think thou hadst been wandering about all last night instead of sleeping here on thy good soft bed."

"All right!" said Zaidos, nodding. He smiled at the speaker the bright and winning smile that always won a way for him. He was on his feet in an instant.

"That's the way to do it!" commended the man. "Wake when you wake, not rubbing thy eyes out."

Zaidos was soon standing in a line in the office while the twenty men in his group answered to name. Then what Zaidos had feared came to pass. A name was called and no one answered. Again it rang out sharply. There was a consultation between the two officers at the desk. The young mountaineer who had led the perilous way through the chained door was gone! Zaidos, keeping his face as free from interest and expression as he could, stood stiffly at attention while the count was made and questions put to the men. As luck would have it, Zaidos was asked but one thing. Had he seen the fellow on his pallet before he himself went to bed? He answered honestly that he had. He was conscious of keen scrutiny from the officers, and knowing of his own escape and return, felt that he must be looking the picture of guilt. The truth of the matter was that his military training in school made him so perfectly at ease and so soldierly in appearance that he was very noticeable in the line of slipshod, lounging, green recruits.

They were presently ordered to drill, and for two hours went through a grilling labor with their arms. Again Zaidos' trained muscles served him well. While he was tired and muscle-sore at the close of the drill, others were on the point of exhaustion. They were sent back to their barracks and flung themselves down to rest.

The incident of the young mountaineer seemed closed. He did not return, nor did the slightest whisper concerning him reach Zaidos. Four days dragged by. Two days were filled with strenuous drilling. Twice Zaidos was visited by members of his father's family—devoted old servants who begged to do something to free him from his present position, and who questioned him vainly for news of Velo Kupenol. On the second visit Zaidos decided to entrust the old servant with the papers which he carried. He opened the flat leather folder in which he had placed them. They were gone! Zaidos was well aware that the packet had been on him since the moment he had received it. He could only think that they had been stolen, while he slept. But why should any one of the ignorant men about him take papers which could not concern them and leave untouched the large

James Fiske

bills folded in the same compartment with the papers? He reported his loss. The officers who had been in charge on that eventful night had been transferred, but the new Commandant was just and obliging. He had a thorough search made of every man in barracks, but the papers were gone. Without them Zaidos felt himself an outcast. He resigned himself to his fate. How foolish he had been to suspect Velo! He should have been the one of course to care for the valuables, yet he could not but remember his father's anger when Velo had suggested it. Zaidos knew his father to be a just and generous man; and he knew that there was some good reason for his distrust and dislike, although the time had been too cruelly short for explanations.

The proofs of his identity at all events had disappeared, and in such a mysterious manner that it seemed hopeless to search for them. Zaidos had always wanted to join the army, but he had anticipated all the honor and pleasure of graduating from West Point, in America. This was indeed the raw and seamy side of soldiering. He was a philosopher, however, so he shrugged his shoulders, gave the old servants the best instructions he could about closing up and caring for the estates, and threw himself, body and soul, into his new adventure.

The third day, while they were drilling, an automobile raced up and stopped with a suddenness that nearly threw its occupants from their seats. It was filled with soldiers, and with them was a little fellow closely bound. Zaidos looked at him with a sinking heart. He had never seen the pallid, quivering face, with its wild black eyes. No, the night had been too dark, but instinct told him that here was the deserting mountaineer. Zaidos looked away. The man was dragged through the doors, and again a thick curtain seemed to fall over the incident.

But a load of apprehension seemed to be cast on the soldiers. They continued to talk about the prisoner in low voices. Not one of them, with the exception of Zaidos, however, realized the true horror. It was war times and at such a period there was but one end for desertion.

Zaidos prayed not to see it. He would not let himself think of it. He threw himself into his work and with his knowledge of Boy Scout tactics and the wonderful range of their knowledge he passed on to his comrades all he had learned before he had left America on the journey which had had such an exciting end. He never once suspected the influence he innocently exerted for good. Boy as he was, he taught the soldiers in his group so much that they were the special objects of attention to their officers. Drill went smoothly and evenly; the men gained poise and assurance. Zaidos was almost happy in his work.

Then suddenly on the fifth day the blow fell. The unbelievable horror came to pass.

Zaidos and his group passed out into the street as usual, early in the morning. As they made formation a smothered groan like a deep breath escaped them.

Against the blank wall before them, bound, stood the deserter.

Once Zaidos had read a highly colored account of a man who had felt the extremest depth of horror. The book said that he had felt as though his bones were turning to water, and Zaidos had sneered at the description. It flashed into his mind when he looked into the wild, chalky countenance of the man against the wall. He glanced down the line of soldiers. A stupid blankness seemed to envelop them. Pale as death they stared at the shaking creature before them. There

James Fiske

was a terrible silence that sounded as loud and beat as fiercely in their ears as the boom of cannon. Things moved with frightful deliberation. It seemed that they stood for hours staring at the doomed man. It seemed to take hours of physical, dragging effort to obey the next command and move directly in front of that ghastly face. Then more moments, hours, or ages, ticked off endlessly with the dull beating of their hearts. In the face opposite a dull despair dawned slowly. Expression died out. A fearful understanding of things washed away all earthly hope. He stared at the file of men in front of him as dumbly as the ox approaching the butcher. He had deserted, he had been caught, he was to die; that was all. All the little simplicities of his life lay behind him. His wife—his little *girl*-wife, the tiny baby, the warm hut, the friendly wildness of the trackless mountains. They were back of him; he could no longer turn to them. Back-to-the-wall he stood, this untrained, undisciplined creature, facing a line of muskets that wavered in the shaking hands of the soldiers. There was not one of them who would not have faced a regiment, untried as they were, for the men of Greece are heroes; but to stand there and aim at that one poor quaking target. * * * It was a nightmare. It was delirium. Zaidos felt his bones turn to water. He almost fell. Down the line a man fainted.

The priest approached and, walking swiftly to the condemned man, spoke to him in a low and tender tone. The man did not reply. He nodded, but looked at the soldiers. The priest, tears coursing down his face, stepped back.

There was a brief command, a rattle of arms, another order, a pause, a sharp word. Then came a snarling report of guns * * * and on the ground before him lay a crumpled heap. Zaidos, sick to the soul, obeyed the order to retire. He had fired in the air!

The day passed in a horrid daze. Two of the firing squad were so ill and shaken that they could only lie on their cots with eyes hidden, and moan. It was the first tragedy that had entered their simple lives.

The heart of Zaidos rebelled. He could have stood the rage and fear and excitement of battle, but this unspeakable act in which he had taken part seemed too much. As night approached he began to fear the quiet hours of the dark. When he closed his eyes he could see that white, blank face before him.

It was with a deep feeling of relief and gratitude then that he obeyed the order to march to the wharves. There were forty men included in the command, and they went off gaily, glad of anything as a change from the barracks.

Three transports waited at the wharves. Zaidos obeyed an order to go aboard the largest, a noble ship ready to put out. It was crowded with men. Zaidos, with two others, boarded her. They were led down and down into the depths of the ship, and with despair Zaidos discovered that he was to be one of the assistant stokers.

The engine-rooms were stifling, notwithstanding the big electric fans that supplied a change of air as it entered through the great air intakes. The furnaces roared. A couple of engineers nodded to him and one of them led him to a bunk where he exchanged his uniform for the thin, scant garments suited to his new work. At once he returned to his new duty. He found the shifts were short, but the work was so heavy and the heat so intense that at the end of his first duty he went to his stuffy bunk and threw himself down, more exhausted than he had ever been in his life. He lost track of time down there in the firelighted gloom, and the clock seemed to bring no understanding to him.

At last night came, and he was sent to his bunk again to remain until summoned. The engineer, who was like an officer in charge, was not a hard man. He understood the necessity of breaking his boys in gradually. Zaidos, too tired to sleep, lay in his bunk watching the men about him and listening to their idle or boastful talk. His native tongue had come back to his remembrance, and it was easy to understand most of them.

Presently he heard groans from the next berth, and a tall soldier came over and looked in.

"What is the matter with you?" he said to the complaining youth lying there.

"I'm sick, I'm going to die!" said a whining voice. "I have been down in the engine-room until I am nearly cooked. I think my back is broken too."

The listening man laughed.

"Not a bit of it, my boy!" he said. "You are tired out. That is what ails you. You have soft muscles evidently. You will be all right soon."

"I tell you I am about dead!" insisted the voice.

Zaidos listened, puzzled. There was a familiar sound in the tones, but for the life of him he could not place the speaker.

"I tell you I am in a bad way!" insisted the unseen speaker. "I shall appeal this matter to the King as soon as we land."

"That's a good idea," said a soldier, nodding. "When I came away I left my tobacco pouch in barracks. I will appeal too. It is not to be endured!"

"You don't understand," said the fellow. "I am Velo Kupenol, the head of the house of Zaidos. I am a Count!"

The tall soldier nodded with a twinkle in his eye. Zaidos fell back in his bunk with a gasp of surprise, and listened.

"Is that so?" said the soldier. "I heard of the death of Count Zaidos the other day. So you are his heir, eh? I thought he had a son. Where does he appear in this story of yours?"

"He is dead," said Velo. (It was he.) "He went to America, and has not been heard from. So I am the heir. I shall appeal to the King, I tell you!"

"All right; all right!" agreed the soldier, while the others, listening near, laughed. "At least it is a pretty story, Count. Stick to it. We like to hear you talk."

"Well, it is so, and I can prove it!"

"How?" said Zaidos, suddenly leaning over the edge of his bunk.

For a full minute Velo stared at him with bulging eyes.

"How will you prove it?" said Zaidos with a steady stare. He leaped to his feet and, shoving the tall soldier out of his way, went to the berth and thrust his furious face close to his cousin's.

"You won't prove anything!" he said in a low, tense tone. "You have made a fool of yourself and of me. I won't have my father's name dragged into this mess. I'm here as Zaidos, the stoker; and you will forget Zaidos of Saloniki as fast as ever you can. And if I find you telling anything more, I will thrash you, Velo Kupenol, within an inch of your life. I can do it, too. I learned that in America, at least. And for the present we are in the same fix. We are here as common soldiers. My papers were stolen from me in barracks the night my father died, Velo, so there won't be any proving at all. We are just a pair of stokers on a transport. But don't think for a *minute* that I mean to stay where I am. A Zaidos cannot be kept in the hold. I shall do something for the honor of my name, you may be assured of that. But remember *I am Zaidos, the stoker.* As I said, if I find that silly tongue of yours wagging, I will make—you—good—and—sorry."

He paused, and with keen eyes searched Velo's face to make sure he comprehended it all.

Velo was silent, and Zaidos returned to his cot, once more conscious of his fatigue and lameness.

But Velo, turning to the wall, pressed his face to the hard mattress, and let the deadly hate he bore his cousin fill his very being. He pressed his hand on the stolen papers hidden in his kit. Zaidos must die. Zaidos must die! All his evil blood boiled in him. For hours, when he should have been sleeping off his fatigue, as Zaidos was doing, he lay hating and plotting. A dozen evil schemes formed in his mind, but Velo was a coward. *He* did not mean to be caught in anything that looked shady. When he was finally rid of his cousin, he did not want to be unable to appeal to the King and later enjoy the boundless wealth and vast estates and unblemished honor of the Zaidos name.

Before dawn both boys were called to go into the engine-rooms with their shift. Zaidos, although lame and aching, was still refreshed by his slumber and ready for work. But Velo could scarcely drag himself along. He worked as little as possible, the engineer grumbling at his poor performance. He kept close to Zaidos, dogging him about like a treacherous and snapping cur.

His chance came finally. Zaidos, with a great shovel of coal, was approaching the terrible open door of the blazing furnace. Velo, with his empty shovel, had just left it. As his cousin passed him he gave a sly twist to the dragging shovel, which threw the corner of it between Zaidos' feet. He stumbled and fell headlong toward the open door where a horrible death seemed reaching for him.

But as he plunged forward, the chief, who was beside him, turned and shoved his rake against the falling body. It was enough to change the direction of his fall. He crashed to the ground safe. He was on his feet instantly, turning to his cousin with a look where certainty and inquiry were mingled. But as he opened his mouth to speak, a sudden jar under them was followed by a terrific crash, and in a moment a fearful list of the great vessel disclosed the worst.

The transport had been struck by a submarine and was sinking. Water rushed into the engine-room and rose toward the immense bed of living coals in the furnaces. There was a savage hiss of steam. The ship listed rapidly to port. A rapid ringing of bells cut the air. The chief listened. It was the danger signal, never sounded when any hope of saving the ship remained.

"Up to the deck for your lives!" he roared, and throwing down the shovels and rakes, the men and the two boys sped for the entrances. They struggled up with a mob of terrified men who pushed and fought. More and more the big boat leaned to the sea. When Zaidos finally gained the deck, one rail nearly touched the water. He thought she would go under immediately, but thanks to some uninjured air chamber below, she hung balanced. On the bridge the Captain shouted through a megaphone.

"Jump before she goes!" he cried. "Swim away from the wreck!"

Zaidos, forgetting all but the present danger, seized his cousin by the arm and rushed him to the side of the ship.

"Jump!" he cried.

"No!" screamed Velo. "No, no! I am going to stay here!"

"Don't you hear the Captain?" cried Zaidos. "Jump! Jump!"

Velo pulled back and Zaidos urged him toward the heaving water.

"It's our one chance, Velo!" he cried. "We will go down with the ship if we stay."

He suddenly gave Velo a push and flung him into the water. Together they swam rapidly from the rail. As though to give the soldiers the one slim chance for their lives, the ship, leaning on its side, still balanced at the lip of the sea. Then with a sickening roar the vessel went down. Zaidos looked over his shoulder. On the bridge, white haired, erect, undismayed, stood the Captain. As the waters engulfed him he even smiled. A fearful force dragged at the boys and swept them toward the great whirlpool made by the ship. They swam desperately, and just as strength seemed to fail, the pressure was released and they floated in a sea covered with wreckage and with swimming or drowning men.

The boys were swimming close together when Velo gave a cry and clasped Zaidos around the neck in a choking grip. At once they both went under, and Zaidos fought his way out of the strangling clasp; but Velo seized him by the arm. They came up, and Zaidos turned on his cousin.

"Don't, don't let me go!" Velo begged with staring eyes. "I'm getting a cramp!"

"Then let go of me!" cried Zaidos. "I'll save you if I can, but don't grab me!"

Velo, overcome with terror, tried to obey, but his reason was not as strong as his terror. Once more he tried to grasp Zaidos.

The boy turned, grabbed him by the throat, and forced him under water.

He struggled furiously for a space, then suddenly went limp. Zaidos drew him to the surface. He was unconscious. He supported the unresisting weight on his shoulder, and as he kept afloat, he despairingly scanned the horizon.

Bearing down upon them at full speed he saw an English Red Cross ship!

CHAPTER IV

A STRUGGLE IN THE SEA

Hope rose in Zaidos' bosom. He gave a sigh of relief. The boat was only a couple of miles distant, and coming full steam ahead. Something bumped heavily against Zaidos' shoulder. It was a dead soldier. A gaping water-soaked wound on his head sagged open, and told the story as plainly as words could do. He was supported by a life belt carelessly strapped around him. The body pressed against Zaidos, bumping him gently as it moved in the wash of the sea.

Still holding Velo with his left arm, Zaidos unbuckled the single strap that held the life belt and the body, released, slipped down into the water and disappeared. Zaidos, treading water as hard as he could, next managed to get the belt around Velo and buckled it. He fastened it so high that Velo's head was supported well out of the water; and Zaidos let himself down in the water with a gasp of relief. He felt that he was good for hours now. Keeping a hand on the strap of the belt, he turned on his back and floated. The water was warm, there was a hot sun shining, and with the Red Cross ship approaching, Zaidos felt that he was indeed lucky.

He felt no uneasiness about the Red Cross ship changing its direction; the sea about was full of wreckage and men swimming and clinging to spars and timbers. It was not as though he and Velo had been alone there in the sea. The Red Cross ship had no doubt seen the explosion and sinking of the transport. So Zaidos floated easily beside his unconscious companion, occasionally calling to some hardy swimmer who came near, and expecting soon to see the rescuing vessel approach. Velo opened his eyes, felt the lap of the waves round his shoulders, and gave a convulsive leap out of the sea.

"Had a good nap?" asked Zaidos.

Velo groaned. "I am going to die," he said.

"Not just yet," Zaidos assured him. "I wish you would have a little more courage," he said crossly. "You are in the *greatest* luck. The transport is gone, with all her officers and nearly all of the men. I don't suppose there are more than six or eight hundred afloat out of the three thousand on board. Look over there, Velo. There is a Red Cross ship coming along. She will pick us up, and then we will be all right."

Velo looked eagerly and gave a cry of dismay.

"Oh, oh, *oh*!" he screamed. "We are lost; we are lost!" He burst into tears.

Zaidos rolled over and looked.

When you are in the water, as every Boy Scout knows, every object afloat looks mountainous. A common rowboat looms up like a three master, and Zaidos, looking in the direction of the Red Cross ship, saw a couple of battleships approaching, while a huge Zeppelin like a great bird of prey floated overhead. How many submarines were playing around beneath him, he could not guess. One thing was clear. They were in a position stranger than any story, madder than any dream. Floating there, almost exhausted in the sea, they were to be in the center of a sea fight. Velo still wept, and Zaidos himself felt a sob of excitement choke his throat.

"We are going to get it from both sides," he remarked to his cousin. "That Red Cross ship is trying to get out of range until this thing is over."

"What is going to become of us?" cried Velo.

"Don't know!" said Zaidos. "And I don't so much care. At least I don't mean to worry. I've watched a lot of poor swimmers go down just from exhaustion; and if we are not rescued, why, we just *won't*, that's all. I'll tell you one thing, though," he said with sudden anger, "if you don't brace up and stop making me listen to your whimpering, I am going to duck you again. I did it before when you were trying to drown us both and I am perfectly willing to do it again. You had better brace up!"

Velo was silent, and Zaidos fixed his eyes on the most amazing sight that a Scout ever witnessed.

Suddenly a wild shot ripped across the water, skipped along twenty feet from them, plowed its way into the sea, then disappeared.

Velo screamed. Another shot followed so close that the wave from it rocked them. Zaidos watched the Zeppelin with fascinated eyes. It circled round and round, in an effort to get over the biggest ship. A shot leaped up at it, and missed. The Zeppelin rose a little, then returned to the attack. Another shot narrowly missed it; but at that instant a bomb dropped like a plummet. It was a close miss. Zaidos could see wood fly as it clipped the prow and exploded as it reached the sea, doing but little damage.

"Look! Look!" cried Velo.

Another battleship was coming, and another, until before
them five great monsters battled. The Zeppelin returned to
the attack, and Zaidos himself cried, "Look! Look!" as a
swift gleam of light across the water, on a line with his eyes,
betrayed the lightning swift course of a torpedo. It struck the
ship, and at the same moment the Zeppelin dropped an
accurate bomb. There was a terrific explosion as the torpedo
struck amidships, a spurt of flame as the bomb scattered its
inflammable gases over the decks, and fire burst out
everywhere. Another torpedo tore into the ship. Zaidos' eyes
bulged as he watched, the monster ship flaming and roaring
with repeated explosions, her own guns valiantly firing to the
last. As she plunged nose-first into the sea, the boys could
see the crew, like ants, pouring, leaping over the side, only to
go down in the vast whirlpool made by the sinking vessel.

The Zeppelin now soared skyward, made a wide circle that
took it almost out of sight, and returned to attack another
ship. Then a strange thing happened. The upleaping shot
from the battleship crossed the bomb from the Zeppelin in
mid-air, and as the bomb exploded on the deck of the cruiser,
the shell from her aeroplane gun hit the delicate body of the
airship and tore through it. As the Zeppelin came whirling
down, turning over and over in the air, Zaidos could see the
crew spilling out like little black pills out of a torn box. That
they were men, human beings whirling to a dreadful death,
did not occur to him. He had lost all sense of human values
in the terrible pageant before him.

It seemed like a picture show, only with the vivid colors of
reality and the deafening noise of exploding shells. Once
they felt the submarine pass under them, so close that it

made an eddy that pulled them toward the combating ships. When it came up to release its dart, the boys were too intent on keeping themselves enough out of the sea wash to breathe, to see whether the torpedo struck or not. The excitement grew in intensity. Gradually the group of fighting ships drew nearer the swimmers. They were not more than half a mile away. Another great hulk went down. The Zeppelin, with broken wings wide spread, floated on the sea. They could scarcely see it except when a wave made by a falling shell lifted some of its delicate framework.

"There goes another ship!" exclaimed Zaidos. "I wish I could tell what they are. I can't see any flags or emblems from here."

"I don't care what becomes of them," Velo said irritably. "I'm water-soaked. I feel queer. I'll never get out of this."

"Oh, brace up!" cried Zaidos, speaking in English. He reflected that Velo could not understand a word of the language, and proceeded to give vent to his feelings in a tongue that he had found extremely expressive in times of need. He glared at the drooping boy, while the guns continued to thunder.

"You make me sick! You make me tired!" he exploded. "Great Scott, you are the worst baby I ever saw! I wish to goodness you were wherever you want to be, wrapped up in cotton batting, I suppose, and tied with pink string, and laid on a shelf in a safety deposit vault. You are a regular jelly fish! I wish I had some fellow along who had a real spine! I—" he paused for breath.

"I don't know what you are saying," complained Velo.

"It doesn't matter," said Zaidos in Greek. "It was nothing of consequence. I think I told you once or twice before just about what I thought about things. If you feel better to whimper around all the time and complain about things, why, so ahead! I suppose we *will* drown. I'm getting pretty tired myself, but I mean to hang on as long as I can.

"If this fight ends before nightfall, that Red Cross ship is sure to come back and pick up all they can, and you can see for yourself just the position it is in now. It can't get to the battleships without coming past us. So we have a good chance. I've been in the water longer than this without much damage. But I wish you could manage to keep yourself together, Velo. I'm sure we will come out all right. I'm not going to die now, before I have a chance to do something worth while." He shook the water from his face.

"Well, I believe they are going to quit," he said. "I wonder how many fellows have seen anything like this. Three dreadnaughts and a Zeppelin sunk and wrecked, and I don't know which is which or who is who. It doesn't much matter to us, however. However long or short I live, I'll never forget it. Never! Just think of it, Velo; three ships of the line, and a flyer." He turned to the opposite direction, scanning the sea with keen eyes.

"Yes, sure enough, here comes the Red Cross! The fight is over. She is going to pass us. That's pretty fine, isn't it, Velo? Don't that make you feel warm all over?"

"She may not stop," said Velo gloomily.

"A Red Cross ship pass all this bunch swimming around here without stopping to pick them up? You are crazy!"

"There are not so very many," insisted Velo.

"They will stop to pick you up if all the rest of us go down before they get here," said Zaidos patiently. "You have the life belt, Velo, so don't worry any more than you have to."

A silence followed. After the wild racket of the guns, it seemed as though the sea itself whispered. On and on came the Red Cross ship. It approached so near that they could see that a couple of boats were being lowered. They were gasoline launches, and they raced here and there, pausing every little while to pick up a survivor. As they approached Zaidos and his cousin, Velo commenced to scream in a weak voice. Zaidos sighed, but said nothing.

When the nearest launch approached them, Velo thrust him back and left him swimming while he, with his life belt, was lifted over the side. But a sailor had Zaidos by the shoulder. It was well, for the boy was at the point of exhaustion, and as he felt himself drawn into the boat, he found a sudden darkness settle over everything, and he sank back unconscious into the arms of a doctor.

When he opened his eyes, he was in the clean, airy, floating hospital. It took a little thought for Zaidos to recollect where he was. When he did so, he made an effort to arise. To his great surprise, he could not move. He threw back the covers. His leg was in splints. He stared at it with surprise.

A nurse came up. "How did that happen?" he demanded. "What ails my leg anyhow?"

"You ought to know," she smiled. "We expect you to tell us. Your leg is broken below the knee. Just the small bone, you know. Do you mean to say you did not know it?"

"I should say not!" said Zaidos. "You are sure it is broken? It hurts a lot, but I don't see how it could be broken without my knowing it."

"Yes, it is certainly broken," the nurse repeated.

"Oh, you are talking English, aren't you?" cried Zaidos with delight.

"Why, yes. This is an English Red Cross ship," replied the nurse. "You are English, are you not? Or American?"

Zaidos shook his head. "No, I'm a Greek," he explained. "But I've been in America at school since I was a little chap, and I have had an English room-mate for three years."

"That's it, then," said the nurse. "You must not talk now, however. You must drink this and sleep if you can. There are a lot of badly hurt men here. *You* are all right, but pretty well water-soaked and tired out. Try to sleep."

She started on, but Zaidos put out his hand and detained her.

"Just a moment, please," he said, smiling at her in his sunny way. "Is there a fellow here called Velo Kupenol? Tall fellow, thin, and looks a little like me perhaps?"

"Perhaps not again," said the nurse, frowning a little. "Yes, your friend is here. He does not seem to have anything the matter with him, yet he acts like a very sick boy."

"Seems to enjoy poor health?" asked Zaidos, smiling. "Well, I myself can't really blame him. You don't know how very *wet* we felt! I feel as though I could lie here a week and enjoy these dry sheets."

"You will be very likely to do so whether you enjoy it or not," said the nurse. "Legs do not mend in a day. When your friend thinks he is strong enough, I will suggest his coming to visit you."

She passed on, and Zaidos lay staring at the wooden ceiling so near his head.

Round and round and round goes the wheel of fate, thought Zaidos.

He wondered what the next turn would be, and where it would carry him. He drank from the cup the nurse had given him, and presently dozed off, although his leg pained too much to allow him to get a sound sleep.

He was aroused later by voices near him, and recognized the sound of his cousin's voice. Velo was talking in a rapid, low tone to one of the doctors.

"Looks like a nice boy," said the doctor in Greek.

"Yes, he is," said Velo. "But if he is my cousin, I must say he is one of the most stubborn fellows I have ever known."

"Is that so?" thought Zaidos, keeping his eyes shut tight. He thought there would be no more talk about him, but the doctor went on, "He doesn't look it."

"No," said Velo, "but he is. I thought I would never be able to rescue him from that sinking transport. He went sort of crazy, he was so afraid, and when the order came to jump, he clung to the rail, and refused to move. I had to twist his hands away, and jump with him."

"Well, I do declare!" thought Zaidos. He decided that he had better find out just what sort of a fellow he was supposed to be anyhow.

Velo went on, "When I got him into the water, I had to take him over my shoulder, and swim for dear life to get away from the boat before she went down. We just made it, and at that he clung to me with such a grip that I thought I would have to let go and leave him to his fate."

"Queer how they hang on to one in the water," said the doctor. "It seems strange he does not swim."

"Oh, he swims a little," said Velo. "He *thinks* he swims well, but it does not amount to much. I got hold of a life belt and buckled it around him, and kept his courage up as well as I could. The fight out there nearly finished him."

"I don't know as I blame him," said the doctor. "It must have been a pretty stiff experience, especially when a shot came your way occasionally."

"Yes, it was exciting," Velo agreed. He spoke with the ease of a man accustomed to worse things. Zaidos wondered how the doctor ever believed it all.

"Well," he said, "I'll have to go on. You can congratulate yourself, young man, on having the courage and patience to stick it out and save the lad. It is a great credit to you and I'm proud to know you." And he turned and walked softly away between the white bunks.

Velo remained standing near Zaidos. Presently he came over and looked down at his cousin. Zaidos opened one eye and looked up. The other he kept tightly closed. It gave him a teasing, guying expression of countenance which he had many times found very irritating at school.

"Dear, *dear* Velo," he said with a simper, "how can I *ever* thank you for saving my life?"

James Fiske

CHAPTER V

INTO SERVICE

Zaidos' method of punishing Velo for the yarn he had told the doctor took the form of an exaggerated gratitude. Being perfectly independent of praise himself, Zaidos could not understand why on earth Velo should have taken the trouble to misrepresent things so. As far as Zaidos could see, there was nothing to be gained by it. The incident was past and did not concern the doctor in any way. Zaidos, who did not know his cousin at all, had yet to learn that his was one of the natures that are incapable of any noble effort, yet which feed on praise. With Velo everything was personal. If he passed a beautiful woman driving in the park, he thought instantly, "Now if that horse should run away, and I should leap out and grasp the animal by the head, wouldn't that be fine? I would doubtless be dashed to the pavement a few times, but what of that?" He could almost hear the lovely lady, pale and shaken, as she thanked her noble preserver and pressed into his hand a ring of immense value. The lovely lady was always a Countess at least, and frequently a Princess.

Velo imagined drowning accidents, and fires where he dashed the firemen aside, and made thrilling rescues of other lovely ladies who were seen hanging out of high windows. Velo himself always came out unhurt and with his clothes nicely brushed and in order. Sometimes he imagined a slight, *very* slight cut on his forehead, which had to be becomingly bandaged, but that was always the extent of his injuries. Velo liked to imagine bandits, too; big, ferocious fellows whom he outwitted, or choked into insensibility in single combat. At a moving-picture show, he always sat in a delicious dream, admiring his own exploits as the pictures flashed on the screen.

Thus it was perfectly natural and simple for him to take the adventure of the previous day, and twist it to his own glorification.

To Zaidos this would have been such an impossibility that he simply could not have understood it at all, even if someone had explained Velo's way of looking at things.

To Zaidos the only possible or natural way to look at things was to do whatever came up for a fellow *to* do, and to do it as soon and as well as he possibly could. Not knowing Velo, he did not dream that he was in the habit of glorifying himself on every possible occasion. If he had, he would have pressed a little harder. As it was, he drove Velo into a cold fury by his sweet, humble gratitude.

"Oh, Velo," he would say, "whenever I think how you wrenched my hands from the rail, and forced me into the water, and swam with me to safety, I don't see how I will *ever* thank you!"

Then he would get out the square of antiseptic gauze the nurse had given him for a handkerchief and cry into its folds as loudly as he dared.

Zaidos had to take medicine to keep down fever, so there were two bottles on the tiny table beside him. He had to take a dose every hour. Once he woke up, and took the bottle in his hand and started to pour it out just as the nurse came past. She gave a look at the bottle, smothered a cry, and snatched it from Zaidos' hand. She was pale.

"How—where—when did you get that?" she stammered.

"What's the matter with it?" asked Zaidos. "Isn't it my medicine? I've been taking it all the time, haven't I?"

The nurse had regained her self-control and even smiled.

"Have you been asleep this morning?" she asked, as though the medicine no longer interested her.

"Just woke up," said Zaidos. "I had a fine nap."

"That's good," said the nurse and walked away, taking the bottle in her hand.

But five minutes later, when she reported to the doctor, her manner was not so calm.

"What do you think?" she cried, closing the door of the tiny laboratory where he was working with an assistant. "What can this mean? This bottle was on young Zaidos' table instead of the medicine I left there!"

The doctor scanned the label.

"Bichloride of mercury," he said. "Why, that's queer!" He pondered. "What do you make of it?"

"I can't make a *guess* even," said the nurse. "There is no one out there who is delirious, and Zaidos could not get up on that broken leg in his sleep, if he wanted to. If it was not such a crazy idea, I should say someone had a reason for getting rid of Zaidos, but he is very popular, and his cousin thinks the world of him."

The incident was mysterious as well as serious. They discussed it and made guesses which flew wide of the mark. The doctor quietly ordered a change of medicine for Zaidos, and removing the bottles on his table, gave the nurse instructions to give him the doses herself. She did so, without rousing any suspicion in Zaidos' open and confident mind, *but Velo Kupenol noticed the change.*

He was more attentive to his cousin than ever.

Only in the rare moments when he was alone and secure from observation did he allow himself to take off the mask of good nature and kindliness, and let those thin features of his twist into the wicked leer that well fitted them. He no longer saw himself in the part of hero. He was too eager to remove from his way the boy who stood between him and all the luxury he craved. But his common sense told him that at the present, at least, there was nothing to be done. He would have to await further developments. In the meantime he would gain his cousin's confidence. That ought to be easy. Zaidos was the most friendly fellow he had ever seen. Velo resolved that if ever he came in for the Zaidos name and title, he would show them just how haughty and overbearing a young nobleman could be. But in the meantime, he thought it better to do as Zaidos commanded and say nothing about the family. Zaidos had elected to be known as a common soldier, and he would keep to his word. Velo realized that he himself could make no pretentions while Zaidos was about; he would not stand for that. So Velo acted in his best and oiliest manner, and waited on the nurse, and urged his services on the doctors, and wondered why they never acted at ease and friendly with him, as they all did with the laughing boy on the cot.

When they were sent ashore it dawned on Velo that now they would be separated. Zaidos would have to go to a hospital to wait for his leg to heal; but he was well, and would be set at some duty which would separate him from Zaidos. That would never do. He worried over it as they approached land, and finally took the matter to the doctor. He put the matter strongly. He had promised Zaidos' dying father that he would not be separated from the boy. They were almost of an age, but he had always been the one to look out for Zaidos, and surely now if ever was the time to be true to his trust. He explained the manner of their enlistment, and reminded the doctor they were both listed among the drowned.

"You see I *must* remain near him," he urged. "Just help me find a way."

"The hospitals are all short handed," mused the good-natured physician. "I think they would be glad to get you. There is lots of heavy lifting that tells on the nurses, and all that sort of thing, you know. It will be two weeks before Zaidos can be discharged. That bone is not knitting right. It was splintered, you see. I'll do all I can for you, Velo, and I think it will work out nicely."

So it came about that when the patients on the Red Cross ship were transferred to the land hospital within the English lines, Velo was there in full force, carrying one end of Zaidos' stretcher. Of course it was the light end; Velo saw to that instinctively, but then it was Velo's attention to just such little details that made life easy for him.

Zaidos soon improved so that he was allowed to hop about on crutches. The second day he used them, however, a brass pin somehow worked into the arm pad and scratched him badly before he knew that it was just where his weight would press it into his shoulder. It was very sore, and that same night, when he sat carefully on the edge of his narrow bed, waiting for Velo to come and help him undress, the bed went down and Zaidos was thrown to the floor. It hurt his leg again. Velo picked him up and was so sorry that for once Zaidos felt a twinge of remorse when he thought of the way he had guyed him.

But the nurse, who had been transferred to the land hospital also, pressed her lips tight together and thought hard. Zaidos was almost too unlucky. She took him under her own special care, although Velo protested and assured her that she must not burden herself while he was there to look out for his cousin.

"I don't see why so many things keep happening to you," she said to Zaidos while she dressed the place on his arm where the brass pin had made a bad sore.

"I *am* playing in hard luck, at that," said Zaidos, smiling. "Every time I turn around I seem to bump myself somehow. I was on the football team, and had won my letter for running. Do you suppose I will ever get to run again?"

"I don't know," said the nurse. "I don't see why this leg should make much difference. It was only one bone, you know, and you could bandage that leg if it felt weak. But you can't keep falling off cots and sticking infected pins into you."

"Funny thing about that cot," said Zaidos. "The bolt that held the spring and headboard together was gone—completely gone. I wonder if it ever was in. Perhaps when they put it together, they forgot that corner, and it stuck together until I happened to sit down on it just right. I've known things like that. I'm glad it didn't go down with some poor fellow who was badly wounded. It gave my leg an awful jolt. And it certainly gets me where I got that pin in the crutch pad. It must have been in the lining, and just worked out. I don't believe it will make a bad sore. My blood is pretty good. It's funny, though."

"A lot of queer things happen to you, Zaidos," said the nurse. "Tell me, have you no other name? Are you just Zaidos and nothing else?"

"Oh, yes, I have five or six other names," said Zaidos, smiling. "But you know in Greece it is the custom to call the—"

He glanced into the face before him with a queer embarrassed look, and stopped.

"Just so," said the nurse. "I understand. You are the head of your house, whatever that is, and you have very sensibly decided to keep it all to yourself while you are mixed up in this war. Well, Zaidos, in England, too, we sometimes call the head of a noble house by his family name. For my part, however, I prefer to think of you simply as a particularly nice, agreeable boy, who has made his illness a very pleasant time for the people who have been near him; and so I think I will call you something simpler than Zaidos. Is John one of your five or six names?"

"Nothing so easy as that," said Zaidos, smiling. "Why, I will tell you what they are."

"I don't want to know," said the nurse. "I, too, have a name that we will forget for the time, but you may call me Nurse Helen. And I have the dearest father in the world whose name is John; so I will call you John. Do you mind?"

"I should say not!" said Zaidos.

"You see, John," said Nurse Helen, "every time I say that name I feel closer to my home and all the dear ones there. Some day I will tell you about them all."

"I wish you would," said Zaidos. "I have often wondered how your people could let a dandy girl like you get into this sort of thing." He wanted to say such a *pretty* girl, but did not quite have the courage to do it. "You know you might even get hurt."

"It's quite likely," said Helen simply. "One has to accept that chance. And there *is* a chance about everything. A lot of the people in this war, dreadful as it is, will go home when it is over, and get run over by London busses, or fall down stairs, or things like that."

"Or slip on banana peels," added Zaidos. "You are right about it. I wonder I never thought of it before."

"Who is Velo Kupenol?" asked Helen. "Is he really your cousin?"

"My second cousin, to be exact," said Zaidos; "He has lived at our house ever since he was a boy eight years old. I don't exactly understand Velo lots of the time."

"I wouldn't think he was too awfully hard to understand," said Helen.

"Well, he is," said Zaidos. "He has been just nice to me ever since I was hurt, but he has done some of the queerest things. And what he told the doctor about what happened the day we were in the water—Oh well, I can't explain it very well!"

Zaidos was too modest to tell Helen that the account had simply been twisted around to Velo's advantage.

"Don't try," commented Helen. "There is one thing I feel as though I ought to tell you. That is, that I want you to watch that cousin of yours. If we are doing him an injustice, we will find it out just so much sooner. Otherwise it pays to be on guard. Just tell me one thing, John. If anything happened to you, would there be anything for Velo to gain by your death?"

Zaidos looked uncomfortable.

"Oh, I suppose so," he said. "Why, yes, to be honest with you, he would gain a lot. But I can't—Oh, he wouldn't be such a sneak! Perhaps I had better tell you all about everything, now you have sort of adopted me."

"Not if you think best not to," said Helen; "but of course I would love to know all about you."

"And I had better tell you," said Zaidos. "You see, I have no relatives at all except Velo, and we aren't too sure of him yet, are we?"

He rapidly recounted the happenings of the past from the time the telegram reached him in far America. Several times Helen interrupted with a keen question.

When Zaidos finished, she sighed.

"Well, John," she said, "as far as I can see, there is not a thing you can take as a real clue. But it all looks queer, just the same. Sometimes everything *will* happen so things look black. That is why circumstantial evidence is always so dangerous. But all the same, I worry over you."

"Don't do that," said Zaidos. "I ought to be old enough to look out for myself."

"What are you going to do when your leg heals?" asked Helen.

"I'm going to join the Red Cross," said Zaidos.

"How perfectly fine!" exclaimed Helen. "We will be posted together for awhile if you do, because the field hospitals at the front where I am going are very short handed. Don't you suppose we could persuade Velo that his duty lies in some other sphere of action?"

"I don't believe so," said Zaidos.

"No, I know we couldn't," said Helen. "He has repeatedly told me that he would never leave you. Here he comes now. Let's try it!"

She smiled as Velo approached and drew himself up. Nurse Helen was undeniably beautiful, even in her severe uniform.

No, Velo had *no* intention of deserting his dear cousin. If Zaidos joined the Red Cross, so would Velo. It made no difference to him at all. If Zaidos was stationed in the trench hospitals at the front, that was where *he* would be found.

And two weeks later he actually did find himself there. It was in one of the lulls between engagements, and they arrived with no more excitement or danger than might attend any summer trip.

But there they were, actually in the trenches.

CHAPTER VI

A LETTER HOME

Zaidos, who was still on sick list and walked with a cane, was nevertheless put to work, in order to familiarize him with the position of the trenches. For two weeks the English had been expecting an attack, and the inaction was telling on the nerves of the officers.

The men are only kept under fire for four days. At the end of that time, they are sent back a few miles in shifts to the nearest village where they find quarters, and rest from the nerve-racking, soul-shaking clamor of guns and buzz of bullets. The trenches were wonderful. Zaidos and Velo, the Red Cross badges on their arms giving them free passage, soon explored every inch until they were perfectly familiar with them all. Zaidos drew a sketch of the plan to send to the fellows in school.

First of all, and nearest the opposing force, is the line of the small trenches for the snipers or sharp-shooters. These men, facing certain death in their little shelters, are picked shots, and keep up a steady, harassing fire at anything showing over the tops of the enemy's trenches or, failing that, at anything that looks like the crew of a rapid-fire gun. These, of course, they guess at from the line of fire as the guns are placed in the first line of trenches in little pits of their own. On his map Zaidos marked the positions of the guns with an A.

Behind the snipers are the barbed wire entanglements, a nightmare of tumbled wires piled high in cruel confusion. Close behind this are the observation trenches. There was no firing from these small trenches; they were simply what the name implied: look-outs. Leaving these, and passing down the zig-zag connecting trench, the first line trench was reached. This was fifty yards from the wire entanglements, and along here the rapid-fire guns were set.

When Zaidos and Velo made their first visit through the trenches, they were puzzled to see that the guns were all set at an angle, so that the line of fire intersected, usually just over the barbed wire entanglements.

Zaidos asked about it.

"We protect our guns in that way," explained the young Lieutenant who accompanied them. "With the fire coming at an angle, it is difficult for the enemy to get the exact position of our guns, and they are unable to follow the line of our fire with their own fire, and so cripple us. On the other hand, you notice that all trenches are either battlement shape or zig-zag."

"I wondered why," said Zaidos.

"Well, that is so a shot from the enemy, no matter what the angle, striking in a trench, will simply go a few feet, and plow into the bank of earth ahead of it. Formerly, a single shot, raking the length of a portion of a trench, would cost hundreds of men. Now it seldom means a loss of more than six or eight."

James Fiske

It was fifty yards between the entanglements and the first line trench, and in the two hundred yards between that and the second line trench, there was quite a little underground settlement.

The bomb-proof shelter was a regular cellar with sheets of steel over it, and earth over that. It was dark, and the dirt walls and floor gave out a damp and mouldy smell. The men had made crude provisions for comfort. Narrow benches were about the walls, a door from some wrecked building had been brought with much labor, and converted into a table, around which the men sat and played cards.

But Zaidos was most interested in the First Aid Station. He felt that much of his time might be spent here in this strange dug-out.

It was a strange mixture of the latest thing in surgical science and the crudeness of the caveman.

The walls were simply scooped out. They might have been dug with a gigantic spoon, so rough they were and so rounding. The floor had been packed, or trodden hard, and in the middle of the small space was a rude operating table. Beside it, however, on enameled, collapsible iron stands, looking as though they might have been just carried out of some perfectly appointed hospital, were rows of delicate instruments.

There had been no firing for some time, and the place was empty. The surgeon and his assistant sat reading a month-old copy of a London paper. They scanned the columns eagerly, and laughed heartily at the jokes. For London gallantly jests, even in war time.

The lieutenant introduced Zaidos and Velo to the doctors,

and explained their presence.

"Well, me lad," said the older man, cordially taking note of Zaidos' sunny smile and fearless eyes, "I'm thinkin' that we need such as you. We can't hope those fellows over there beyond will keep still much longer, and we will have the deuce of a time to hold our position, I believe. Of course we will do it, but it will mean a lot of work for us in here, worse luck!

"You want to familiarize yourself with every turn of the place. A lost moment may mean a lost life, perhaps yours, perhaps the man you are trying to help. You may have to leave the connecting trench you are running along and take to the top of the ground. If a shell falls ahead of you, you will find your path stopped up. Have you ever been under fire?"

"I don't know just what you would call it," said Zaidos laughingly, and proceeded to tell the doctor how they happened to be in their present position.

"Well, well, well!" said the doctor. "You ought to do! First drowned, and then shot at, and submarined. It does seem as though you ought to be able to keep your head, with only a few simple bullets and gas bombs flying around."

He got to his feet stiffly, for living underground makes men rheumatic, and put down his paper.

"Just pay attention," he said in a crisp, business-like way. "When you serve wounded men, remember two things. Work deliberately, yet with the greatest speed. Many a man has died from one little twist given in getting him on his stretcher. Forget the fight, forget everything for the time but that the torn body is in your hands. Do you know anything at all about lifting a man?"

"I do," said Zaidos. "I'm a Boy Scout. Besides, we learned all that at school."

"Good!" said the doctor. "All you have to do is to remember what you know, when the necessity of using your information arrives. When you have your man on the stretcher, get here as soon as ever you can. Don't wait for anyone; private and General alike must stand aside for the Red Cross. Wonder if you could stop a cut artery?"

"Yes, sir," replied Zaidos.

"How?" said the doctor, reaching out his arm. Zaidos took it and demonstrated the thing and the doctor gave a grunt of satisfaction.

"When you get your man here, lay him down on one of the benches or on the floor or anywhere else that you see a place for him. Don't wait, for we will attend to him after that."

"Yes, sir," said Zaidos. He foresaw lively times.

"Good morning," said the doctor, sitting down and taking up his precious paper. The boys went out, feeling as though they had been dismissed from class.

The large cook house was very close to the First Aid Station, and was equipped with wonderful field stoves and great kettles and pots. A number of cooks were in charge, and the boiling soup smelled good enough to eat!

Three zig-zag trenches led from the cook house and First Aid Station to the second line of trenches.

Here was a repetition of the first line trench, machine guns and all. Back of it stretched a line of snipers' trenches, and behind them another barbed wire entanglement. A tunnel led under this; several of them in fact, and large enough to permit the passage of a number of men at the same time. This was arranged in case the line was pushed back by the advancing enemy.

When Zaidos had arrived at this point in his drawing, his paper gave out, and he was obliged to write the rest on the back of the sheet.

"You will see, fellows," he wrote, "just how the second trench is laid out by looking at the first. Back of the barbed wire and the observation trenches come a lot of connecting trenches again. These are not laid out in exactly the same direction as the first group, of course, but are generally the same. Instead of a shelter for thirty men, there is a shelter for one hundred thirty men. The cook house is much larger, and the First Aid Station is really a sort of hospital, where the men can be placed until they are taken back to the regular field hospital which is back of the third trench, four hundred yards away. This makes the hospital proper pretty safe.

"The shelter for men in the third position holds three hundred men easily and the hospital is quite complete.

"You never saw such courageous fellows as these are. Just think, you chaps, kicking as you do over there about the feed and the beds and the barracks, what it is like to live underground against the bare earth!

"The men are never able to undress to sleep. Once in two weeks each man has a bath, which he has to take in *two minutes*. He is then given a complete set of new underwear. The men spend four days in the trenches, almost always under fire night and day. There has been no firing since we struck the place, but there is going to be a bad time soon, they say. And then the noise is perfectly deafening, they tell me.

"When the men have been four days in the trenches under fire, they are sent back in squads to the nearest village for four days to rest and get their nerves back in shape.

"I was talking to a jolly young Englishman this morning, and he told me about the place he stayed in the village. He has just come back.

"He was quartered in a cellar, where they were perfectly safe from Zeppelin bombs or stray shells, but it was dark and damp and cold. When he went to sleep at night the rats ran all over him, and he and all the other fellows had to wrap their coats around their faces to keep the rats from running over the bare skin. Some rats, eh?

"A lot of chaps go to pieces with rheumatism, and have to be sent way back to the stationary hospitals in the cities.

"This Englishman I was talking to was over in France last Christmas, and he told me all about the time they had. Seems queer, but I think it is so. He said almost every fellow in the outer trench had some sort of a Christmas box with fruit-cake and candles, and 'sweets' as he calls candies. There they were, wishing each other a merry Christmas, and shaking hands, and laughing, and the snipers' guns popping away at the Germans a few feet away from them. Pretty soon a white flag went up in the enemies' trench, and they ran one up, too, and stuck up their heads to see what was what. They didn't know if it was a ruse or not; but there was a group of Germans sitting on the edge of their trench with their legs down inside ready to jump; and they were calling 'Merry

Christmas, Englishmen!' as jolly as you please.

"Well, that was all our fellows needed, and they got out of their holes and advanced. But one of their officers went first, a young fellow who was pretty homesick on account of the day, and he went up to a big German officer, and they agreed that there should be a truce for the day, and shook hands on it. So the men came across and met, and tried to talk to each other and learned some words from each other. The Germans had Christmas boxes, too, and they swapped their funny pink frosted cakes for the English fruit-cake, and gave each other cigarette cases and knives for souvenirs.

"Then it came dinner time, and they brought their stuff out on the neutral ground, and ate it together. Then pretty soon they all went back to their own trenches, and commenced singing to each other. The English sang their Christmas carols, old as the hills of England; and the Germans boomed back their songs in their big, deep voices. I tell you, fellows, it must have been queer! Just before dark, the German lieutenant stood up once more, with his white flag, and the English officer went to meet him. The German talked pretty fair English and the men heard what he said.

"'We have a lot of dead men here to bury,' he explained. 'Will you come and help us?' So the English said yes, and they all came out again and helped to bury the fellows they had shot. Then they all stood together, and the German officer took off his helmet and everybody took off their caps, and the German officer looked down at the graves, and then up, and he said, 'Hear us, Lieber Gott,' and the fellow said he must have thought his English was not good enough to pray in; so he said a little prayer in German, but everybody sort of felt as though they understood it, and of course some did. And then he put his helmet back, and shook hands very straight and stiff with our officer, and said, 'Auf wiedersehn,' and turned away. And everybody shook hands and went back to their own trenches, and long after dark they kept calling to each other 'Good-bye! Good-bye!'

"Well, fellows, that was the end. Next morning they were peppering away at each other, struggling like a lot of dogs to get a throat hold. Seems sort of queer, don't you think so?

"I don't believe this could happen now, because they have been fighting so long that they hate each other now. I think at first that they were like dogs that someone sicks into a fight. They do it because they want to be obliging, or because they think they have to mind. They would just as soon stop and wag their tails and go to chasing cats or digging for rabbits together. But they have fought now until the bitterness of it has entered deep. I can't guess what the end will be. I don't believe anybody can.

"You had better stir up everybody over there about it, and 'rustle the requisite' as Main always said. *Everything* for field hospital work is badly needed. Seems to me you could send a few hundred dollars of stuff over, well as not. You, Corky, you had better sell that car of yours. You know the Commandant doesn't half approve of it, and Baxter can give up that motor-boat. You will drown yourself, Baxter, sure as sure! And think how much better you would feel to stay alive, and help a lot of shot-to-bits poor fellows in the bargain.

"Things look so different when you are right on the ground. What they tell me about some of the shot wounds that come to the hospitals makes me wonder if I have enough backbone to stand up under it, when the fighting really commences. I believe I am getting scared!

"The English fellow told me that after the first shot or two you didn't seem to mind anything; you just went right ahead, and tended to work as though, as he said, it was a May morning in an English lane. I suppose he thought that was about as near Paradise as he could imagine, but the finest place *I* can think of is—Oh well, fellows, you know. I wish I was close enough to the gang to have you pound me on the back, and to kick that big brute of a Mackilvane for trying to stuff me under the bed. I'd like to hear some of Gregg's rag-time, and see Mealy Jones try to ride the bay horse.

"But this is the end of my paper, and I've got to go back to the hospital. To-morrow I am to be put on regular duty. That's why I am writing you this long letter. It may be a good while before I write another; so good-bye, old pals. I'll come back some day if I live.

Yours,
ZAIDOS."

James Fiske

CHAPTER VII

A BIT OF ROMANCE

Zaidos sent off his letter and continued his explorations.

He managed to slip away from Velo finally and was greatly relieved. Somehow everything went along better without Velo tagging at his heels. Zaidos felt ashamed when he tried to analyze his feelings. He was at a loss to understand himself. Even Nurse Helen, who frankly confessed to Zaidos that she disliked Velo, was obliged to say that there was nothing openly objectionable about him. His manners were easy and graceful, and he was quicker to jump to her assistance than any man on the detail.

He treated Zaidos with a protective fondness that was almost funny. He watched him, saw that he went to bed and arose on schedule time, helped dress his scratch, and looked after him generally like a faithful and devoted nurse.

Yet Nurse Helen pondered. She never once let him handle one of the dressings which were rapidly healing the ugly little tear in Zaidos' arm. Zaidos, escaping from Velo's watchful eye, felt like a glad little, bad little boy who has run away from school and who refuses to think of supper time, when he must go home and find that father has the note teacher has sent home by some *other* little boy. He went here and there, his sunny smile and ready kindliness making friends everywhere.

Wherever he sat down to rest some soldier told him something of interest. Gunners explained the watch-like perfection of their guns. Snipers told thrilling tales of long shots. The cooks showed him how cleverly the big field stoves came apart, and how they could be assembled at a moment's notice.

At supper time his new friend, Lieutenant Cunningham, called him. He had kept a place for Zaidos beside him. Velo had been omitted from the group, so he smilingly sat down in another bend of the trench with his pannikin of stew and cup of coffee, seemingly quite content. But black hate raged in his black heart!

Velo was a strange sort. He was a coward; he dreaded danger and endured hardships badly. Yet the thought that harm might come to him never entered his head. He was deeply superstitious, and while he could and did change the bottles and place the poison within his cousin's reach, while he placed the rusty pin in the crutch where it would inflict a wound on Zaidos' body, while he could plan endlessly to rid himself of his cousin, he would not *himself* directly aim the blow or fire the deadly shot. He rejoiced in the battle that was threatening. Zaidos would die, and he wanted the evidence of his own eyes. Also he wanted the statements of witnesses. Sometimes when he heard Zaidos' ready laugh, and saw his bright, straightforward look, a flicker of pity shadowed his dastardly resolve. Then he remembered the soft living, the ease and luxury of the house of Zaidos, and remembering that he, as Velo Kupenol, must be all his life nothing but a dependent on his cousin's bounty, he steeled his wicked heart to its self-appointed task.

But he must change his tactics. Zaidos as usual was surro-unding himself with friends. Velo felt that he must be doubly careful. There must be no more strange, unaccountable accidents to Zaidos. When the blow fell it must crush him utterly; until then, he must be left to move securely.

Velo thought of all this as he sat talking to the soldier beside him and eating the plain fare of the men in the field.

The talk was all of the coming attack. Spies had reported a movement of preparation in the enemy's ranks, and there was a stir of warning in the very air. To Velo's amazement, no one seemed worried or anxious. The conversation moved smoothly on, as though the battle was a test of skill on a chess-board. Not a man there seemed to regard the coming event in a personal light. Even the uncertainty did not distress anyone. The attack would surely come, but whether it would come the following night or in a week's time did not seem to matter in the least. Velo had expected to see in an event like this a lot of men brooding gloomily over the possible outcome, a dismal time with last farewells, and touching letters written home. He watched the young officer beside him. He had finished his meal and had taken out a pad of paper and an indelible pencil. He wrote rapidly, but with a calm and smiling face. Velo could not imagine any tragic farewells in *that* letter.

Velo, still staring at the writer, listened to the conversation along the wall of the trench. It had at last turned from war to out-door sports. Velo, who never exercised if he could avoid it, listened idly. A small, pale boy in a lieutenant's uniform was violently upholding certain rules while the officer next to Zaidos disputed him smilingly. They argued pleasantly, but with the most intense earnestness.

"Who is that straw-colored chap?" Velo asked the writer

beside him.

"Across?" questioned the scribbler. "We call him 'Sister Anne.' You know she was the lady in Bluebeard's yarn that kept looking out the window. He is always sticking his head out of the trenches, to see what he can see. He's going to get his some day."

"Don't you know his real name?" asked Velo. "He acts as though he thought he was somebody of importance."

"Why, when you come down to it, I suppose perhaps he is when he is at home," said the man. "He's a jolly good sort, though. He's the Earl of Craycourt."

"And who is the chap beside my cousin?" asked Velo, steadying his voice with difficulty.

"The Prince of Teck's second son," answered the writer. Velo's curiosity rather disgusted him. "Anybody else you would like to know about?"

"Well, who are you?" said Velo, trying to get back.

"Your very humble servant, John Smith," he said. He slid the pencil down into his puttee and stood up, bowing. He did not ask Velo for his name but, closing the pad, strolled off and slid an arm around the neck of the second son of the Prince of Teck.

Velo for once felt small, but he jotted young John Smith down on his black list for further reference! As for the others, he could not get over the fact of their noble birth. He stood staring at the group. Zaidos was as usual in the center of things, having the best sort of a time. That was Zaidos' luck, thought Velo. He stared at the bent head of "John

Smith," bending over the "second son of the Prince of Teck." For a plain "John Smith" he seemed exceedingly chummy with the young nobleman. Velo was a natural-born toady. True worth, real nobility of mind and soul meant nothing to him. But he did not lack assurance. After a moment he braced up and joined the group where Zaidos and Lord Craycourt, who answered willingly to the nickname "Sister Anne" were swapping school yarns and the others were in gales of laughter.

And at that moment, without warning, in the arm of the trench where Velo had just been sitting, a great shell dropped and exploded with the noise of pandemonium. A wave of dirt and splinters were pushed towards them. As the air cleared, there was the sound of a feeble moan or two, then silence. "John Smith," rather white, stood looking at the fresh mound of earth.

"There were six fellows in there when I came away," he said. "Get to work, everybody!"

With sabers and pieces of wood and hands, they cleared away the wreckage. One by one they came to the pitiful fragments that had been men. One by one, they laid them reverently aside. It was only just as they had reached the angle leading to the cook house that they found a crumpled body that moved slightly as they touched it.

"We can't hurt him much; he's too far gone," said "John Smith." "Lift him up, and get him over to the First Aid!"

They kicked a rough into the cook house, hurried through it and the connecting tunnel to the First Aid. There they laid the shattered body on the table, and with the exception of Zaidos and Velo, all went back to repair the trench.

Never again during his experience with the Red Cross did Zaidos find time to watch the marvelous skill of a field surgeon. The soldier, a large and muscular man, was almost in ribbons. His flesh was actually tattered, and the dirt had been driven into the wounds. A leg had been blown off, and both arms were broken. Yet he lived. There was quick and silent work for awhile. When the doctor finally stood up and looked critically at his finished task lying there bandaged like a mummy and breathing with the heavy slowness of insensibility, he nodded in satisfaction.

"I only wish all the other poor fellows who come in here had your luck, my boy," he said, nodding at the insensible patient. "If I could get you one at a time, it would be an easy matter; but when you come at us by the dozen, it is a different affair entirely. He's ready," he added to Zaidos. "Get a couple of bearers, and take him to the rear. Don't lift him yourself. There are plenty to do it to-night, and your leg is not too strong yet."

Zaidos called a couple of privates from the trench, and went with them back to the main hospital. The man on the stretcher lay like dead. Nurse Helen received him.

"I'm coming your way to-morrow, John," she said. "I have been detailed to the First Aid shelter."

"I'm sorry," said Zaidos. "It is too near the firing line in there for a woman."

"For a woman perhaps," said Helen with a little smile, "but not for a nurse. That is a different thing, John."

"I can't see it," said Zaidos.

As he spoke, another dull roar marked the falling of a

second shell.

"I don't see why they start up to-night," said Zaidos. "I wonder if that did any damage."

"They want to worry us enough so that the men will lose sleep," said a soldier standing near. "But no one will bother about a few shells. The men will get into the bomb proof shelters until daylight. It is a waste of ammunition as it is."

An orderly entered with a written call for a nurse for the First Aid Station. Nurse Helen was called to the Head Nurse and in a moment came hurrying back to Zaidos.

"They have sent for me now," she said. "I suppose some other cases have come in."

"I'll go back with you," offered Zaidos, and together they stumbled along through the rapidly gathering dusk.

Three more men had been hurt, and when they had finally been sent back to the hospital, it was almost midnight.

Zaidos found Helen sitting at the opening of the shelter, looking up at the stars. She made room for him on the plank.

"I'm thinking hard about home, John," she said. "One's viewpoint changes so. I wish I knew that I have done right to come here and leave my parents and little sister. I'm just *so* lonely and troubled to-night that I have half a mind to tell you my story."

"I wish you would," said Zaidos, "if you *feel* like telling me. I told you all about myself, and it would make me feel sort as if I was really am old friend of yours if *you* told *me* things, *too*."

"Of course," said Helen. "I know how you feel. Well, John, you know, don't you, that we are certainly in for an attack as soon as it is daylight? Perhaps before, because the enemy has searchlights that make it easy for them to bother us in the dark. I know they are expecting a big battle because this is a much coveted position. A great number of fresh troops are on the way here. I learned that to-night, and that looks serious, because we have our full quota of men here now. They are going to change shifts all night. So there will doubtless be heavy work for the Red Cross people, and much of that may be field work. And, John, it may be that never again will you and I sit talking together."

"Nonsense!" said Zaidos. "Don't talk like that! You are too sweet and pretty to die, and *I* can't die because I have got such a lot to do."

Helen shook her head. "I don't say that we will," she said. "But boys as busy as you, and women nicer than I could ever dream of being, have gone out into the dark—crowds of them, in this war."

Zaidos saw that she was deep in one of the black moods that sometimes comes over the sunniest natures.

"Well, never mind," he said. "You are going to tell me who you are, and all about things, and we are going to have the nicest sort of a visit, if we sit up all night."

"I shall have to sit up anyway," said Helen. "I'm on night duty."

"Well, then so am I," said Zaidos, "so begin!"

"Our home is in Devonshire," said Helen. "My father is rector of a large parish there. Everything for miles and miles around belongs to the Earl of Hazelden. He has three children, a girl and two boys, and we grew up together. We liked the same sports, and enjoyed the same pleasures. The daughter, Marion, who is only a year younger than I am, went to school with me near London, and afterwards to France where we were perfected in languages. My sister is four years younger than I, so in those days she did not really count. I forgot to say that my mother was well born, and had a large fortune in her own name, so we were able to live better and have more luxuries than a clergyman can usually provide. Of course we lived simply, but we could afford the best and most exclusive schools, and I had horses to ride that were exactly as good as the Hazelden children's.

"At last Marion and I returned from school, our education finished. Ellston Hazelden, the eldest son, was in the army, of course, and Frank, the second, was in London studying law. At Christmas Ellston came home on leave, and Frank came down from London. Oh, John, I wish you knew Ellston! He is the finest—there is *no* one like him! Of course *any* girl would have fallen in love with him. I did. Oh, I did indeed! I shall never see him again, John, and I am not ashamed to tell you how I loved him and how I will always love him."

"Well, then—" interrupted Zaidos.

She silenced him. "Let me tell you the rest. I loved him, and when he told me that he loved me and wanted me to marry him, it seemed the sweetest, most natural thing in the world. I suppose here you think will come in the dark plot of the simple rector's daughter, and the haughty Earl who thinks she is not good enough for his son and heir. It was not a *bit* like that. Lord and Lady Hazelden were adorable. They came and welcomed me with open arms, and Lord Hazelden said he had been planning it ever since we were little tots!

"John, it just seemed as though they could not do enough for us. Lady Hazelden was in deep mourning for her mother, so we decided not to announce our engagement for six months. Then in three months more we would marry. Every day the Hazeldens drove over with some beautiful plan for our happiness. They had one entire wing of the castle done over for us. Ellston came down often as he could."

Helen lapsed into silence, and sat staring into the night.

"Well, what then?" asked Zaidos, staring at the lovely, sorrowful face beside him. "Did he die?"

"No," said Helen haltingly. "We quarreled."

"Quarreled?" echoed Zaidos. "Quarreled after all that? I don't see how you could!"

"I don't see now, either," said Helen. "It was my fault. I should have *made* him make up with me."

"What was the fuss about?" asked Zaidos. He was intensely interested. He had never been so close to a real love affair before. Of course he had met a girl at one of the hops; the one he gave the collar emblem to. Zaidos couldn't think of her name, but he remembered that he had been pretty hard hit. He knew she was a pretty girl; funny he couldn't think of her name! It occurred to Zaidos that a fellow ought to know a girl's name anyhow if he was crazy over her. And he had been quite crazy over her for a whole evening. Had it *bad*! Anyhow, he was sure she was a blonde. That was proof that he remembered and suffered! But Helen was speaking.

"I hate to tell you," she said. "It seems so trivial now."

"Well, let's hear about it," said Zaidos. "Perhaps we can get hold of the chap and fix things up."

"Not now," said Helen sadly. "It is too late. There always comes a time when it is too late, John. Don't forget that. I have found it out."

She paused again, and Zaidos was afraid she was never going on, but finally she took up her story.

"There is actually nothing to it. It commenced with the color of a dress I wore. Tony said it was the most unbecoming thing I had ever had on. I had just been visiting a friend in London, a very advanced girl, and she had been telling me what a mistake it was when one gave up to the prejudices of a man. She said do it once and you would do it always. So when Tony said quite calmly, 'Do please throw the thing away, or burn it up,' I thought I ought to take a *firm stand*. I said, 'I shall do neither. This is a *perfectly new dress*, and I mean to wear it all summer.' Tony laughed. He said, 'Well, I'm blessed if I take any leave until winter then!' Of course he was joking, and a girl with the least common sense would have known it; but I retorted, 'That is an excellent plan!' He said, 'Why, Helen, you don't mean that, do you?' and I said I certainly did. We parted rather stiffly. It was his last evening at home, and I had put on the frock in honor of it. He wrote as soon as he reached London, and referred to the dress again. He said such trivial things should never be permitted to come between two people who loved each other. I returned that it was not trivial, but a matter of principle, which I should support. John, it actually parted us. Actually parted us! Just think of it!"

"Well, I never heard such bosh!" Zaidos said. "Why didn't you write and tell him it was perfect nonsense, and that you were sorry?"

"That is the worst of it," said Helen. "I did just that, and told him how I loved him, and that it didn't matter *what* I wore, so long as he liked it. Oh, I said everything, John, that a silly and repentant and loving girl *could* say, and sent the letter to his quarters in London. I even put my return address on the envelope."

"What did he say?" said Zaidos.

"Not a word!" said Helen sadly. "Not one word! I waited for two weeks, and then he was ordered to the front. Still he did not write. I sent him back his ring; it was all I could do, and left home for awhile. He came down for a day, but did not come to our house. Not a very exciting affair is it, John?"

"Perfect bosh!" declared Zaidos. "I'll bet anything, *anything* that he never received your letter at all, or else he answered and you did not get his letter. Why didn't you telephone him? *Letters* are no good."

"I asked him to telephone me," said Helen. "I watched that telephone for three days all the time."

"Didn't you leave it at all?" said Zaidos.

"Only once for an hour," said Helen, "and then I had my own maid sit right beside it.

"That is all there is to my poor little story, John boy. Tony is somewhere in France, if he still lives, and I came out here when I could stand it no longer at home. You see I am not afraid of death because I don't in the least care to live without Tony."

"Well, it's too bad," said Zaidos. "Wish I had been there. I just know he never got your letter. I just know it!"

"The story is ended now, at any rate," said Helen. "If Tony lives he will go back home and marry some woman who has common sense to appreciate him, and as for me, to the end of my days, I shall be just Nurse Helen." She sighed softly, and for a moment looked into the night.

"Do you want to see him?" she asked. She drew from her uniform a slender chain with a big gold locket swinging on it. A crest was on it set with diamonds that flashed in the dim light. Zaidos looked at the open, handsome face.

"Look like him?" he asked.

"Exactly like him!" she replied.

"Well, when I meet him," promised Zaidos, "I'll tell him a few things!"

Helen smiled. "You will never meet," she said. "But if ever anything happens to me, John, take this and send it to him. You'll remember the name, won't you?"

"Oh, yes!" said Zaidos, "I'll remember! But just you take notice, he never got that letter!"

"What a stubborn boy you are!" exclaimed Helen.

"Not stubborn at all," declared Zaidos, looking at the lovely face. "I'm merely a man *myself,* if I *am* young."

CHAPTER VIII

HAPPINESS FOR HELEN

Again Helen laughed.

"All right," said Zaidos. "Have it all your own way, but I know I am right about this affair. A fellow with a face like that, engaged to a girl like you, would have acknowledged that letter just in common politeness if nothing else. Just to say, 'Thank you, but I don't care to play with you any more!' Oh, yes, he would have answered it!"

"Whether he would or not," said Helen, "the breach is too wide to cross now. It is all over. I deserved to lose him and I feel no bitterness about it. My fate is what I deserve."

Zaidos hated to hear her self-reproaches. "I don't know about that," he defended awkwardly. "Probably he ought to have come half way. It looks so to me."

"It is growing light in the east," said Helen. "We have talked all night about my poor little affairs. Let us think of something else now, let us—"

She was interrupted by a shattering boom of artillery. It seemed to crack the very air. They sprang upright and stood

James Fiske

for a moment listening.

"The beginning!" said Helen solemnly.

"Well, good-bye," said Zaidos. "I must see where they want me to go. Where's that doctor?"

The doctor and his assistants as well were there. They hurried into the dug-out, calm, collected, business-like.

"Set out the antiseptics, nurse," said the doctor. "You were on night duty, but I can't let you go until someone comes to relieve you. This is very apt to be a big day. You, Zaidos, get out in the first line trench, and don't lose your head. That cousin of yours is hunting for you. I sent him forward too. Nurse, the new troops are here; every trench and shelter is full of men. A big day, children, a big day!"

He rubbed his muscular, sensitive hands together. Another roar shook the ground and balls of dirt rolled down the walls of the First Aid Station. They heard the muffled beat-beat of feet running through the trenches toward the front.

Zaidos, shivering, his teeth chattering with excitement, buckled on his aid kit and bolted out with a last wave of the hand. He hurried over through the short trench into the cook house, and then made his way along the trench toward the front. A return fire was beginning now, and high in the sky was seen the first Zeppelin. Like a great bird of prey it circled high in air above the lines. Then from somewhere in the rear an English airship skimmed to meet it. The bull-nosed Zeppelin soared and the lighter machine followed, light as a swallow. Zaidos stared, fascinated. He could see spurts of smoke from one and then the other. Another delicate craft passed overhead and joined the first English ship in pursuit. Zaidos stumbled on, still trying to watch the chase. He was suddenly thrown violently to the ground, and covered with earth. Screams of agony came from the trench ahead. He scrambled to his feet and ran forward. A dozen men, tumbled together in horrible confusion, lay tossing and shrieking. Zaidos turned faint for a moment. They were the awful flat, senseless cries of hurt animals. "A-a-a-a-a-a-a!" they shrilled and some of them tore at their wounds. Zaidos ran for the nearest man and knelt beside him. He tried to turn what was left of his body, and could not. He glanced around for help. Sneaking past toward the rear he saw a familiar figure. It was Velo Kupenol. Zaidos called him sharply, and the stern note of authority made Velo turn.

"Come here quickly!" commanded Zaidos.

"I can't!" panted Velo. "Zaidos, it makes me sick! I'm going to the rear for a little while."

Zaidos looked up at the face, white with cowardice.

"Come here!" said Zaidos. Still kneeling he pointed a small but business looking revolver at his cousin's heart. "Come here!" he ordered.

Velo obeyed, the look on his face changing from white terror to black hate.

Zaidos saw the look, and read it with unconcern.

"Come here, Velo!" He held Velo's shifty eyes. "You get to work here. If you don't, I shall shoot you, just as I would shoot a dog. There is no time to talk. Get to work! You hear what I tell you. Turn this man!"

Velo shudderingly put himself to the horrid task of lifting the bleeding and torn body. Zaidos talked as he worked in a

James Fiske

deep, earnest tone that carried to Velo's ears even in the noise of battle.

"I'm going to be after you every minute, Velo Kupenol! You won't disgrace me if I can help it. Go get your stretcher. If you drop it I will kill you!"

He spoke so fiercely, and with such meaning, that Velo felt that for once his easy-going cousin had the upper hand.

As the doctor had said, they were suffering for lack of help, so Zaidos could not afford to let the coward run away. He *had* to have assistance if he was to save some of the lives which he felt were in a measure entrusted to him. So Velo had to be used. He stopped the gush of blood from a dozen wounds and, lifting on one end of the stretcher, ordered Velo, with a nod of his head, to lead on toward the First Aid Station.

Almost immediately they had the wounded man on the table, and again were off. The guns roared. Shrapnel dropped and exploded, or exploded in air. Overhead Zaidos was conscious that the duel in the clouds still went warily on, but he could not give it a glance. He lost all track of time. He saw others with the Red Cross badge, working, working with the same feverish haste with which he kept at his task. A sort of dreadful haze came over him. He labored with desperate haste, with strong certainty and sureness of touch, but he seemed to feel nothing of human anguish or human sympathy. He was a machine set in motion by the pressing needs of battle, and he went on and on in a haze. Men died in his arms or were transported to the First Aid where the doctors and Nurse Helen worked with incredible swiftness and skill.

He did not speak to Helen, nor did she notice him. Velo, still pale, kept doggedly at his task, only an occasional gleam of hatred lighting his eyes when he had to look at his fearless cousin. He was more than ever like a treacherous dog, watching, always watching for its chance for a throat-hold.

And somehow, without a spoken word, the thing became clear to Zaidos. All at once he knew how deeply and utterly his cousin hated him. He knew as well as if Velo had shouted it aloud that he meant to be the instrument of his death in some way or other, sooner or later. And Zaidos, filled with the frenzy of the battle, did not care. He was not afraid of Velo. He put him aside as though he was something that might be attended to later.

A sort of mental illumination came to Zaidos. He cared for wounded men with a quick skill that he had never known that he possessed. He grew so weary that he staggered under his part of the stretcher's load. His leg pained him so that it was like a whip, keeping him awake and at work when all his body cried to drop down and sleep.

Once when he waited in the opening of the First Aid shelter, he was conscious that someone asked, "Have they broken our lines?"

"Not quite, but they are through the barbed wire. Our troops are massing along the first trench."

"If we can hold out until dark we are all right," said the first speaker, a captain with one leg gone at the knee, awaiting his turn with the doctor without the quiver of a muscle.

"The chaps over there beyond are pretty well tired out. I can tell by the way they are fighting. They are trying to save men."

Zaidos hurried out and lost the rest. It seemed to him that the whole world was in conflict just ahead there. The bomb-proof shelter was crammed with reserves. On and on and on went the fighting; for years and years and years it seemed to Zaidos. He did not know that the day waned and night was near. All he knew was that at last, while he and Velo waited in the First Aid for the stretcher to be emptied, silence fell, a silence punctuated with scattering explosions. The darkness had ended the fighting, and the enemy had only reached the first line of trenches.

"It is over!" said the doctor, glancing up.

Velo sank down on a plank and covered his face with his hands. Zaidos, standing, closed his eyes.

"Let those boys rest for five minutes," ordered the doctor.

Nurse Helen gently pushed Zaidos down on a bench. He toppled over and she put a folded cloak under his head. Then for thirty happy minutes he lost consciousness of everything. When an aide shook Zaidos awake, he came to himself with as much physical pain as though his body had actually felt the shock of wounds. He groaned involuntarily. Velo was sobbing dryly from fatigue and pain.

"Come, come, boys!" said the doctor. "Finish your good work! Here, take this." He mixed something in a glass, and gave it to Zaidos, and then repeated the dose for Velo. It braced them at once, and after they had visited the cook house and had taken some hot soup, they prepared to go out on the field again and look for wounded.

The night seemed very dark as they stumbled along. The dead lay piled everywhere in hideous confusion. There seemed to be no wounded. Man after man they scanned with their flashlights. The unsteady lights often gave the dead the effect of motion. As they sent the ray here and there they thought they saw eyes open or close, arms move, legs stretch out, or mangled and tortured bodies twist in agony. But under their exploring hands the dead lay cold.

They reached the first line trench and passed beyond it. Here lay ranks of the enemy, mowed down under the pitiless English fire.

"There is someone living over here," said Velo. "I heard a groan."

They turned and found a group of men; three dead, and across their bodies two who surely moved.

Zaidos propped his light on the breast of one of the dead soldiers and lifted the head of a young officer whose shattered leg held him helpless. He was quite conscious, and spoke to Zaidos in a weak whisper.

"I'm gone!" he said. "See what you can do for the man lying on my leg. I would have bled to death long ago if it hadn't been for his weight."

Zaidos looked in his kit anxiously. It was almost empty and the bandage was all gone.

"Velo, get back to the station and bring me a fresh kit," he ordered. "I'm going to hold this artery until you get back, and see if I can't keep a little blood in here." He sat down and pressed a finger on the fast emptying vein. With his free hand he held a flask to the lips of the almost dying man. Velo disappeared in the dark.

"Really, my dear chap," said the wounded officer, "it's a

waste of time for you to do that. I wish you would jolly well leave me for some other chap. I'm done; and I don't care in the least, so you need not trouble your conscience about me."

Hurt to death as he was, the officer smiled; and Zaidos was all at once filled with the conviction that he was someone whom he had met. But where?

"That's nonsense!" said Zaidos. "We will fix you up if you will make up your mind to hang on to yourself."

"I've been hanging on for a good while," said the officer pleasantly. "I've been here for a year or two, I think. I only came down from London for the night, you see. Not very long, eh, old chap?" He nodded his head.

"You what?" said Zaidos stupidly.

"London, you know," said the officer. "I came down right away. I couldn't be sure it was true. Seemed sort of unofficial, don't you know?" He smiled again. Zaidos understood. He was delirious. He went on muttering disjointed sentences which Zaidos paid no attention to; but every time the man smiled his gay, light-hearted, unconscious smile, Zaidos felt the strange sense of acquaintance. He could see that the man was almost gone. He had lost almost all the blood in his body, and Zaidos did not dare to move him, nor even shift the weight of the unconscious but living man who laid across the shattered leg. Zaidos felt sure that he would die before Velo returned. And he was still more convinced that the man was at his end when after a few moments of stupor, he opened his eyes quite sanely and looked at Zaidos.

"That was a pretty bad blow for me, wasn't it, old chap?" he said quietly. "I think I won't make out to stop much longer. I've been here since eleven this morning. Pretty long for a man hurt like this. I am glad you ran across me. There's a lot of papers in my blouse. Would you mind sending them to the address on the outside envelope? And I wish you would write to my father. Tell him it's all right. Tell him not to let Frank enlist if he can help it. He's too young. And if you can mark the place they put me, it would be a mighty kind thing. Mother would be so glad if she could have me safe in the church at home, some day. Will you do this?"

"Of course I will," said Zaidos. "But I think you have got a chance."

"I don't want it," said the wounded man. "I could not fight again, and there are reasons—I really don't care a hang about living. Just send those letters for me. And one thing more," he tried to lift his hand to his throat, but was too weak. "Will you kindly take off the chain under my blouse," he said, "before anyone else gets here?"

Zaidos felt for the chain with his free hand, still pressing the artery with the other. As he found the chain, a large locket was released from the man's blouse and, swinging against his buttons, sprung open. Unconsciously Zaidos looked at it.

"Send that with the rest," said the officer. He closed his eyes.

"Here, you!" cried Zaidos. "Quit that! Don't you *dare* go and die! Do you hear me? Don't you do it! Do you hear? I want to talk! I don't need to send this anywhere. If you just hang on, you will see her! *Helen is here*! Don't die now! You want to see her, don't you? I know who you are! You are Tony Hazelden!"

"Helen here?" gasped the man.

"Yes," said Zaidos. "She is a nurse over there, a few

James Fiske

yards away."

"Helen here?" said the man again.

"Yes, I tell you!" cried Zaidos. "Hang on to yourself! You want to tell her why you did not answer that letter she wrote you; don't you?"

"I never received a letter," said Hazelden, for it was he.

"That's what I told her," said Zaidos. "Now you just hang on to yourself. Don't you let go! Do whatever you like afterwards, but don't make me go back there and tell her you have gone and died before I could get you in hospital. I'd like to know where that Velo is with my kit! Here, take another drink of this!"

He pressed the flask once more to Hazelden's white lips. The man seemed sinking into a stupor. Zaidos watched him with secret terror. After the miracle of finding Hazelden here, when he was supposed by Helen to be far off in France, and after the brief joy of thinking that he might be the one to reunite the parted lovers, it was too hard to face the loss of his man. Zaidos kept calling him by name. Finally—it seemed a long, long time—Hazelden opened his eyes again.

"I can't see just how it is," he said. "Are you sure Helen is here?"

"Yes, she is here, I promise you," said Zaidos. "And you want to brace up for her sake. For her sake, do you understand? Her heart is about broken. Don't you go and die now after all the trouble you have made."

Hazelden gave Zaidos a straight look.

"What are you thinking of?" he said in his weak whisper. "You don't suppose I could die *now*, do you?"

"Here's my kit," said Zaidos, as Velo came hurrying up.

He fastened the artery rudely but well, and lifting off the unconscious soldier, they carefully placed Hazelden on the stretcher. Many, many times that day Zaidos had been thankful for his steel muscles and man's stature, and now he was more thankful than ever. With all the care possible they carried their burden over the rough, uneven ground back to the First Aid Station.

Zaidos' heart sang within him. The impossible had happened. He was bringing Tony Hazelden back to the girl who loved him, and Hazelden loved her. Zaidos knew that, not only because of the picture Tony carried, but because no one could have seen Hazelden's face when he spoke Helen's name and not know that his heart was breaking for her. Zaidos knew that Hazelden's life hung on the merest thread, but he stoutly believed that his love for Helen would keep him alive until he reached her, at least, and after that Zaidos was willing to trust Helen to do the rest. Zaidos watched his helpless burden with anxiety as they approached the shelter. When they arrived he gave the word to Velo and they gently lowered the stretcher to the ground.

"Stay here a minute," he ordered Velo, and slid down into the underground room. There was a lull in the dug-out as all the men had for the minute been cared for and sent back to the rear, which always is done as much as possible in the darkness.

The doctor and his aids, resting on the hard planks that served as seats, sat upright against the dirt wall, sound asleep. Nurse Helen stood at the white table cleaning the instruments. Zaidos scarcely recognized her. She was haggard and worn as a woman old in years. Color, energy, life itself seemed to have been drained out of her in the terrible ordeal of the past day. Zaidos hesitated. He was filled with fears all at once. It seemed so like planning the meeting of a couple of ghosts. Hazelden, unconscious and at the point of death, and Helen fagged out, worn, and looking like an old woman.

He went to her, tenderly laying a stained hand on hers.

"Helen," he said, speaking rapidly, "I've no time to break the news to you. The most impossible sort of a thing has happened. You have got to hear it all at once, because there is a man almost dying out there and I've got to hurry. You know the reserves that came in to-day? Now hang on, Helen! Captain Hazelden was with them. Oh, Helen," as she wavered and almost fell, "if you go to pieces you will always regret it!"

"Dead?" she murmured.

"No, but he's outside awfully shot, and he has been keeping himself alive just to see you. You will have to help, Helen, if you can."

He left her standing beside the table. She could not call the doctor. She could not speak. They came in with the stretcher, and as she saw its ghastly burden and gave a quick professional glance at his maimed body, the tender woman and the trained nurse struggled for the mastery. The nurse won. Swiftly she prepared the table, called the doctor and helped to lift him from the stretcher.

Zaidos and Velo left to rescue the man whose weight had kept the captain from bleeding to death. His scalp wound was serious but not dangerous, Zaidos decided, and they returned to the First Aid with lighter hearts.

The room was empty. Hazelden was not there. Zaidos' heart dropped. Had he died?

Helen answered the question in his face. She came to meet Zaidos. Her eyes shone, her cheeks were the loveliest pink. Her step was light.

"Well?" said Zaidos.

"More than well!" said Helen. "Oh, John, it is wonderful! Wonderful! And you brought me my happiness! I am to be transferred to the field hospital tomorrow, where I can nurse him myself. He will live; he *must* live! We could not talk, but he knew me. And I know everything is all right!"

"Certainly it's all right!" said Zaidos. "Didn't I tell you so? I knew just how it would be," and the hero of a single ballroom looked as wise as only a fellow could who had been dead-crazy over a girl all one evening.

"What are you going to do about things?" asked Zaidos. "Go on being engaged?"

"Indeed I'm not!" said Helen as she bathed the soldier's head. "Not at all! Just as soon as he can hold my hand, we will be married by the chaplain. I'll never, never risk another misunderstanding!"

"See that you don't!" said Zaidos quite gruffly.

CHAPTER IX

VISIONS

While Zaidos, aided by Velo, continued his heart-rending task among the dead and wounded on that bloody field, now applying the tourniquet to some emptying artery, now administering, drop by drop, the stimulant needed to hold life in some poor fellow, hurrying back with others on their stretcher, or giving way to the fearless and pitiful priests who moved among the dying—while all these things happened, it would be well to pause and reflect on the wise preparation which had made it possible for Zaidos to do well his allotted task.

As a Boy Scout, and in the extra work of school, he had taken a keen interest in the Red Cross work. Zaidos was the sort of a fellow who takes a keen pleasure in doing things well. He stood well in his classes always, not for the benefit of school marks, but because he thought that if he studied at all, he might as well be thorough about it and try to get at what the "book Johnny," as the boys called the textbook writers, really was driving at. It was the same with athletics. He had jumped higher and run faster than anyone else in school, not so much because he was quick and light and agile, but because, having found out that he could run and jump and put up a good boost for the team at other sports, he practiced every spare moment he could find. Zaidos was always trying to see if he could break his own records. He got a lot of fun out of it. It was like a good game of solitaire. He was not dependent on some other fellow. The other fellow was incidental, a sort of side issue and like a good pace-maker. Of course you had to beat him, but the sport was in coming in ahead of your own time.

It was for this that Zaidos had always worked. It had kept him from feeling the petty jealousies and envy which retard the progress of so many of the fellows. Racing with himself, in Red Cross drills, or running, racing, riding or studying, his rival was always present, always ready and willing to take another "try" at something. It was like having a punching bag in his room. Every time he passed it he took a whack or two, and developed his muscles accordingly.

So, in this unexpected and supreme test of his life, Zaidos found himself fit. As the work went on and on, endlessly as it seemed, Zaidos found that his brain commenced to work independently of his hands. The unbelievable wounds of war no longer shocked his deadened nerves. His hands worked more and more accurately and rapidly, but on the inside of his brain was a sort of screen on which flashed the moving picture of his life.

They started from his little boyhood, when he first crossed the ocean up to the time of the last crossing, at the sad summons which had taken him to his dying father. No real moving picture, thought Zaidos, had ever been screened with so many thrills and exciting incidents as the real life-film through which he saw himself rapidly moving. Here and there on the bloody field he puzzled it out for himself, finding that the plot was complete, and that Velo, his cousin, must be the villain.

Zaidos was still ignorant of the fact that Velo had stolen the papers, but that Velo hated him and would be glad enough to get him out of the way grew clearer and clearer, in spite of the apparent friendliness with which he had treated him up to the present time. But now, hour by hour, Zaidos was conscious of a sort of sour look of hatred which seemed to grow plainer and plainer in Velo's sharp face. Zaidos had an uncomfortable feeling that he must keep a watchful eye on Velo. It was nothing but an instinct, but even so, he felt it, and feeling it, was ashamed.

So the time wore on.

Bending over a soldier with a gaping, bloody hole in his side, Zaidos turned to the hospital corps pouch spread open beside him, and felt for a roll of gauze bandage. One little roll remained.

"Get back to the hospital and get another outfit of gauze and tape," he ordered Velo.

Velo stood up and straightened his back. He looked down at Zaidos, then his gaze traveled to the unconscious soldier.

"What do you bother with him for?" he said heartlessly. "It's no use. I'm going to quit. What's the use of working myself to death?"

"Going to desert?" asked Zaidos coldly. He was holding the hurt soldier in a position where he could treat the wound quickly.

"I suppose so," said Velo. "This isn't my fight!"

"Look here," said Zaidos, "I don't care what you do. If you desert and are caught at it, and are shot, it is no affair of mine. I wash my hands of you. But for the sake of your own manhood *get me that bandage* while I take care of this man. Don't be such a *cad*, Velo! Get me the things I need, and then let's talk this thing out later. But don't do anything to disgrace the family. After all, you know, if anything happens to me, why, you are the head of the house."

Zaidos glanced suddenly up at his cousin, and surprised in his face a look that once and for all swept away all the kindly doubts he had cherished. Velo's countenance was so full of cold speculation and deadly hatred that Zaidos started. Then he pulled himself together, and looked Velo in the eye.

"Get the bandages!" he said coldly and Velo, as though controlled by some superior force, turned to do as he was told.

As he hurried across the rough, blood-stained field, he too saw pictures in his mind. He saw the contrasting fates, either of which he thought might be his. The obscure life of a poor relation, dependent on a relative's kindness, and the life of luxury if all that relative had should come to him. A better boy could have planned to build up a career for himself, but Velo could not or would not. He was like a thief who would rather steal the dollar which he could go to work and earn honestly.

Velo had become desperate in the last few days. As he hurried on, he was seized with a sudden determination to end everything. He went into the First Aid shelter and secured the bandages from the supply table and went back, a dreadful resolve taking form as he went. He found Zaidos still bending over the wounded soldier.

"Well, you hurried, didn't you?" he said, looking up with a nod of thanks as Velo handed him the bandages. He went on rapidly, securing the gaping wound so that they could shift the torn body to the stretcher.

"It's funny," he said as he worked, "that we don't run across the doctors oftener out here. Of course they are all at work just as hard as we are, and a good deal harder, poor fellows, but it does seem as though every time we get hold of a case that is a good deal too hard for us to tackle, why, then there isn't a soul in sight to help. I'm so afraid of doing something that will make somebody heal wrong, or limp or something."

"Be a good way to take revenge on somebody," said Velo.

"Why you—" Zaidos could not finish. "How the deuce do you *ever* think up such stuff? For goodness' sake, don't say it to me! You make me sick!" He bent over his patient again, and Velo looked idly about.

At his feet lay a revolver. He picked it up. It was loaded. Idly he tried the trigger. It worked. He looked at Zaidos. How he hated him! They seemed all alone on that field of dead and dying. The tide had swept away and left them there with their work.

There was a sudden red mist over Velo's sight.... Kneeling in the light of the big flashlight, Zaidos loomed up, a clear, clean cut figure with the velvet blackness of the night behind him. Velo brushed his hand before his eyes. Zaidos was putting the last pin in the neat dressing he had applied to the wound. There was a thread of hope for the man. Zaidos smiled. Velo knew he would get up—

The revolver sounded like a cannon. Zaidos, unhurt, got to his feet. He pressed a hand to his side. Velo watched him with fascinated eyes. Zaidos looked down. There was a cut across the service blouse between his sleeve and body, right under his left arm.

Zaidos stared first at Velo, then at the revolver still in his hand.

"How did that happen?" he demanded in a low, tense voice.

Velo swallowed and cleared his throat.

"The thing went off," he said huskily.

"Well, it came near doing for me," said Zaidos, still staring suspiciously at Velo. "You let me have that revolver! Yon are too funny with things to suit me."

Velo, still pale, smiled a wry, twisted smile. "I'm sorry," he lied. "I don't see how it happened. It must be out of order."

"Give it to me!" said Zaidos, "and take the front of this stretcher. I've got to look out for accidents, it seems. I never saw anything so careless in my life. You have just got to be careful, Velo! I won't stand for it! This isn't the first time I've nearly come to harm through your *carelessness*, if you want to call it that. I tell you I won't stand for it! Mind, I don't make any accusations; and I don't claim you are to blame for a lot of things that have happened to me lately, but if things don't stop, why, you are going to be sorry! There won't be any revolvers going off, and your bed won't go down, and your medicine won't get exchanged for poison, like it sometimes happens. I shall just take you out back of the next wire entanglement, and I will give you a *good beating up*, Velo. I remember I used to have to do it when we were about four years old. It used to do you a lot of good, and I suppose all these years since you have had no one to keep you where you belonged. I won't do this, you understand, unless you get careless with guns and things again. You hear, Velo?"

Velo made no reply.

The two boys carefully bearing the stretcher tramped along in silence.

"You hear, Velo?" said Zaidos again. "Honestly, the more I think of it, the madder I get!"

"You stop your nonsense!" said Velo suddenly over his shoulder. His voice took on a whine. "What makes you act so, Zaidos? I'm your cousin, and I should think you would be ashamed of the things you say to me, just as if I haven't stuck right beside you every minute, and as if I had not done everything in the world that I possibly could do to help you. You don't treat me well, Zaidos!"

"I do, too," said Zaidos, stung by this injustice. "I should think I did; but how do you treat me?"

They reached the entrance to the First Aid Station and gave their unconscious burden into the hands waiting to receive him. The doctor scanned the wound.

"Well, boys," he said, "you have saved this man all right." He turned the bright light on the still, white face. "My heavens!" he exclaimed.

"Who is it?" asked the nurse.

Velo looked at the face, and spoke before the doctor could reply.

"I know him," he said. "His name is John Smith."

The doctor was working rapidly with restoratives.

"John Smith?" he repeated. "This is the Prince of Teck's oldest son, and his brother was killed an hour ago. We must keep this fellow alive," he went on, doggedly. "First time I met him he was just an hour old. He won't go out of this world yet if *I* can help it!"

The boys went outside and for a moment sat down on the ground to rest.

"What do you suppose made him do that?" said Velo musingly.

"Do what?" asked Zaidos.

"Why," said Velo, "I asked what his name was one night and he said John Smith. I think that old doctor is making a mistake."

"What does it matter?" said Zaidos. "He would make just the same effort to save the plain John Smiths as he would to save the princes of the world."

"Pooh!" said Velo, sneering. "I guess not! Why should he? He knows a thing or two and you will find it out some day. Why, nobody does anything for anybody unless they get paid for it somehow or other!"

"Oh, say," said Zaidos, getting up and striking one clenched, fist violently into the other, "I wouldn't have your little bit of a soul for anything on earth! I wouldn't have your mean, little bit of a suspicious, ungenerous mind! I hate to remind a fellow like you of anything so fine, but how about my father? What pay, *pay*, mind you, did he ever get for taking care of *you*? What did he ever get for starting that colony of sick people up on the mountain back of his hunting lodge, with a doctor right there, and a nurse or two paid by father?

James Fiske

Do you suppose it made him feel good to see them tottering all over the preserve where he could no longer shoot, for fear of hitting some of the poor wretches?"

"No," agreed Velo, "he didn't get a thing out of all that, and I always thought that colony for the sick was the silliest thing I ever heard of. I'll tell you right now when I get hold of things—" he caught himself up quickly. "I mean, of course, when *you* get hold of things, if you do as I would do, you will send those people packing back to their slums as fast as they can go. As far as his doing for me, why, I'm one of the family and he sort of had to. It is a duty. Besides, do you suppose it was very much fun sticking around that house, quiet as the grave, *nothing* going on, *no* one coming to see your father but old, grey-headed men and women forever fixing up charities?"

"That's all right," said Zaidos. "Do you know what I am going to do as soon as I get out of this? I'm going to cut right back to America and study as hard as I can. Then as soon as the war is over, I will come back here and straighten everything up. I will of course keep the title. You can't give that away, and I wouldn't want to. I'm proud of my name. It is an honorable one and it has been kept clean by the men before me; but I mean to give Greece everything I can turn into money. Then I'll take enough to start me, go back to America again, and cut out a career for myself. I'm going to be a doctor and as good a doctor as ever lived if study will do it. *That's* the monument I mean to give my father and my mother."

He gave a jerk of the head toward Velo, who sat upright before him.

"How does that strike you, old top?" he asked and climbed down into the First Aid pit.

Left alone, Velo sat thinking. Then he rolled over on his face and beat the earth with his fists. Once more the films flew along, in the moving picture of his mind. He saw the wealth of the Zaidos house—gold, gold! a *stream* of gold flowing and flowing *away* from him! He saw the bright lights, the dancing, drinking, all the carousels he had so often dreamed of, slipping out of his grasp. What possible hope could a fellow like himself have of keeping on the right side of anyone like Zaidos? He smiled when he thought what Zaidos would say if he could know or guess what Velo's life had been. What would he do if he ever found out how he had treated Zaidos' long suffering father? And Velo did not try to deceive himself. He knew perfectly well that back there in Saloniki, there were people who would jump at a chance to get even with him, and who would give Zaidos an account of meanness and wrong-doing that would cause him to kick Velo out of the house.

Velo began to hate himself for the uncertainty in putting off what to him was a disagreeable necessity. Once more he went over the situation. It seemed as though he had gone over it a dozen times, a million times. It all ended at the blank wall which was Zaidos. Zaidos *must* be removed.

Now it is a well-known fact that we are what our thoughts make us. Our minds are like our houses, our homes. We do not have to entertain unwelcome guests. We do not have to invite them there. It may be that we feel obliged to treat everyone whom we meet at our games or in school or at work with common politeness. No matter how we despise a man, we can't very well go up to him in the street and say, "Here, I don't like your style," and proceed to knock him out with a good right-hander. Naturally it won't do. But we need not give the bounder the freedom of our homes. So with our thoughts. It is only when we bring them in and grow intimate with them, and make them part of ourselves that they begin to harm us.

Velo, too evil and too lazy to close the door of his mind on common thoughts and low desires, had grown more and more like his unworthy guests. And now instead of kicking the whole mob into the outer darkness, he lay there, face down, listening to their evil whispers.

"Get rid of Zaidos," they said over and over. "Get rid of him. Who will know? Don't you hate him? You ought to! Just because he is the one who really owns everything, is that any reason why you should get out and work for an honest living? You don't want to bother with an honest living. You want to live soft and lie easy. Get rid of Zaidos! Now is your chance! It is your only chance. You know how he makes friends everywhere. He is straight as a string. He does not lie. He wouldn't do a mean action. Fellows like us are afraid of that sort. Get rid of him. Now—now!"

So the whispering in Velo's mind went on, and he listened and listened, and presently he sat up. On his face was written what is written on every man's face when he gives the keys of his soul over to Evil.

Zaidos came climbing out.

"Well, the doctor is going to save your friend Smith," he said cheerfully. "Good work, too! One of the nicest fellows I ever knew, that Smith. Too bad about his little brother. I never saw two fellows so crazy over each other. It seems they are the last of the family. Doctor says this fellow will never be able to fight again, but he will get perfectly well in time. I don't believe it myself. I don't believe any of the men wounded go will ever get all over it, but we can hope so, anyhow. You see I feel as though I knew this man Smith real well because he knows a schoolmate of mine,

Nickell-Wheelerson his name is. He was just a plain boy when we were at school, but he came over with me, and now he's a lord. Poor old Nick, how he will hate it!"

Zaidos paused, and stared into the night.

Velo scanned him under lowering brows.

"Get it over soon—soon!" whispered the impatient Evil in his soul.

Velo put a hand on his breast where the papers were hidden. Zaidos stooped and tightened the strap of his puttee. Velo watched him sneeringly. Zaidos was so maddeningly unconcerned. Velo wondered if he could be near anyone who hated him as he hated Zaidos and not feel and fear it. The urge of Evil became like a heavy hand knocking on his heart. He almost feared Zaidos would hear it. "Now—now—now!" it went.

"Come on, Zaidos," he said, standing up. "Let's get to work. I suppose we have an all-night task before us."

Zaidos yawned. "I thought so, too," he said; "but it seems they are looking for a bad day to-morrow and we have been relieved from duty for the night. A new shift goes into the field in ten minutes, and we go back to the rear to one of the farm-houses there to rest until ten to-morrow. Come on, let's start."

"To-morrow, then," whispered Velo to the Evil in his soul.

CHAPTER X

VICTORY

The boys walked slowly back, picking their way as well as they could in the darkness, occasionally taking to the zig-zag trenches when the surface paths were too obscure. Every-where men were sleeping, rolled up in their blankets and lying uncomfortably along the bottom of the trenches or out on the ground under the stars. The boys did not talk. Zaidos was busy thinking of the present, with all its tragic incidents, and occasionally a funny happening to lighten the gloom. He thought of Helen, and wondered how her well-beloved patient was progressing. He had a sort of "hunch" as the fellows at school used to say, that Helen was a happy girl, and certainly, if the man was conscious at all, he was happy, too.

About four hundred yards from the lines they found the farm-house to which they had been sent. It was practically a ruin. The roof was gone, excepting over one room where a fire burned in a big fireplace, and where a great kettle swung on a heavy chain. This room had had one side blown out of it, so it was not much better off except in the matter of a rainstorm, than the other rooms that had four sides but no ceilings. It was too open to the weather for much use, however, and the small group of soldiers present were quartered in a cellar close by.

A young sentinel showed Zaidos and Velo the way down, and they rolled up in their blankets and tried to sleep. It was a difficult thing to do. Zaidos found that the steady tramping and kneeling of the day and evening had made his leg, so recently healed, ache badly. It throbbed and he turned and twisted in an effort to find a comfortable position.

Velo's head ached splittingly, and he lay staring into the darkness, keeping company ever with the evil thoughts in his heart. He slept finally, however, and did not awake until Zaidos shook him by the shoulder and told him it was time for breakfast. The three-sided room with the fireplace had been turned into a kitchen, and the cooks were busy there when the boys went over. The meal tasted good, and although the coffee was thick and muddy, the boys partook of it eagerly. It was at least hot and sweet.

Velo gritted his teeth with exasperation as Zaidos strolled out and at once spoke to a soldier who sat by the door with a couple of letters and papers in his lap. It was so exactly like Zaidos to get acquainted without a moment's delay. He smiled at the soldier, and in reply the young fellow made a place for him on the bench.

"Sit down, won't you?" he said. "Mail has come, and I got more than my share."

"Glad you fared well," said Zaidos, taking the offered seat. "I see you have a paper. May I look at it?"

"Certainly!" said the soldier. "There is nothing in it. The war news is so censored over home now that you can't get any-thing much out of the papers. I like 'em because I can read the home advertisements, and see notices of people I know, and watch what's playing at the theatres. Makes me forget this rotten hole for awhile."

"That's so," agreed Zaidos. "But just think how crazy all the people at home must be all the while to hear from you fellows at the front."

"I think they are," agreed the soldier. "I have a brother in France, too, and father has just sent me a letter from him. It's fun to compare experiences. Want to read it? You may if you care to."

"Of course I'd like to!" said Zaidos with his ready friend-liness. "There is no one to write to me anywhere except some schoolmates over in America, and I don't suppose I will hear from them for months." He took the closely written sheets of thin paper, and read the letter, appreciating the spirit in which it was offered him.

"My dear Father," it ran. "I received your letter and note last night, and Auntie's parcel the night before. Thank you both very much for same. It is good of you to us both, but do not spend too much money. Hard times are coming on, I imagine. The kippers were grand. Six of us had a great tea on them in the wine cellar of a shattered farm-house where we are for four nights after four days in the trenches. Then we go back to the fighting line for another four days and nights. This place we are at, in the cellar, is a keep with emergency stores and loop holes, and is armored. Twenty-five of us have to keep it at all costs, should the enemy come over the line, which is perhaps four hundred yards away. The bally place is overrun with rats. They run all over your body and head at night, and I have to sleep with my overcoat tucked over my head to prevent them touching the bare skin.

"Up at the trenches, I was four days and nights stationed

about sixty yards from the Huns doing sentry on and off day and night the whole time, waiting with bombs and bayonet in case they attempted to take it, and now on return here have done three more night-guards and then no more sleep again hardly for four more nights, when we return to the firing line.

"It is a hard life, isn't it? For in between, one is sent off on all sorts of fatigues, drawing rations, sand bags, trench boards, etc., etc.

"I must some time see that new Turkey carpet. The only one I see now is sand bags. If there is a big move shortly, which seems more than likely, it may delay our leave as I guess all the troopers would be wanted in that case, but I am looking forward tremendously to seeing you all again.

"Must conclude now, dear father.

"Much love to all from your son,
DICK."

"P. S. We dug up some dead Prussian Guards the other day. There has been some great fighting here and may be again. I don't know what I should do without the candles and matches you send me. They keep me going nicely.

"I have just thought perhaps my letter does not seem very cheerful; so I must tell you we have lots of fun in between the serious parts of the game. Last rest, I had some great French feeds (for about one franc) in a town near by. Got pally with six French gendarmes and hope to see them again when I have another spell off.

"I guess they could take me around the town if I wanted to see the sights. Also at all villages where we stay, I make friends with some of the cottagers, and get lots of coffee and salads and washing done for me. I am getting quite a reputation for finding places to obtain a little meal to vary the Army rations.

"Cigs are best in tins; in boxes they get very damp. Cheer on! Good luck to you.

DICK."

Zaidos handed back the letter with a smile.

"Thank you very much," he said. "That's certainly a fine letter. It was nice of you to share it with me."

"That's all right," said the boy. "Everyone is glad to read every other fellow's letter out here, whether he knows anything about the people or not. We get so few letters. The people at home send us candles and matches and kippers, as you see from the letter, and they send lots of cigarettes to my brother. I don't smoke. They send us paper and envelopes, too. You know all our letters are opened, don't you? I don't see that it makes much difference. I've always thought that I could see how I could write a pretty innocent looking letter if I was a spy.

"They have had a lot of trouble with spies at Verdun, where my brother is. Why, would you believe it, the Germans have come right inside the French and English lines in broad daylight to do their spying! One bold ruse they worked, just once was to rig up one of their automobiles to look like our ambulances. That car carried six Germans, all dressed as English soldiers, and once inside our lines they went dashing around as aids and orderlies.

"All went well with them, they had seen the whole layout and gone down to the very last trench, when one of them stumbled and out came a thoughtless 'Mein Gott!' for he thought he had broken his ankle. Now of course that would have been a catastrophe indeed, but so was that slip into the German tongue. A kindly Providence saw to it that an alert Tommy had heard, and in a trice those six make-believe English soldiers had been rounded up and were on their way to headquarters. Next morning there was a sunrise party, for those Germans must be taught it isn't ever healthy for them inside our lines."

"Indeed they must!" agreed Zaidos heartily.

"We have got to beat them in the end," said the English soldier with the quiet sureness that has so often helped England to victory. "But they are sure as sure that they will beat us, so they keep hammering away and they will keep it up just as long as their men last."

As if in answer to his last statement a shell struck the earth twenty yards away, and exploded. Another followed, and fell in almost exactly the same place.

"See that?" said the Englishman. "Two days ago one of our best guns was there where those shells have fallen. How did they know just where it was stationed? We had not fired it. And it was ambushed from the airships. Pretty rotten, work, eh?"

As he spoke, a snapping, long-drawn snarl punctuated by deeper roars told that the rapid-fire guns and the howitzers were awake along the English lines. A stir of preparation passed like a wave over the resting and lounging soldiers. Two great Zeppelins appeared overhead. They wheeled closer and closer. Even at so great a distance, the roar of their engines was terrific.

Zaidos turned and shook hands warmly with the soldier whose letter he had shared.

"Good-bye, and good luck!" he said heartily. "Hope we will meet some day again."

"Good-bye to you!" cried his new friend.

Zaidos, calling Velo, jumped into the trench and ran along its uneven zigzags, on and on, the roar of battle sounding ever louder, until he reached the cook house, and turning into the arm leading to the First Aid Station, he raced into the room and reported to the doctor.

Velo was at his heels. Once more the evil in Velo's soul was crying to him, shouting to him, "This is your day—*this is your day*!"

"I won't forget," commented Velo aloud; and Zaidos said "What?"

They buckled on their aid kits, seeing that they were supplied with everything. They wore orderly kits now. They contained chloroform in a case, a roll of wire gauze, a long rubber bandage, and a tin which contained vials of hyperdermic solutions. These were only for the use of the field surgeons whom they chanced to meet and who frequently had to call on the Red Cross orderlies and stretcher bearers for supplies. Then in the next compartment was the hypodermic syringe, and beside it a flask for aromatic spirits of ammonia. There was a knife and a pair of surgical scissors. After having dropped his scissors a dozen times or so, Zaidos had taken the precaution to tie them to his pouch with a long, fine string.

There was gauze, eight packets of it; four first aid packets complete, six bandages, and two diagnosis tags and pencils. When there was time, it was sometimes advisable to tag the wounded men. It made them get moved quicker when the patient finally reached the operating room.

A spool of adhesive plaster was perhaps one of the most useful things included, and there were pins and ligatures, and a small pocket lantern which Zaidos at least had never had occasion to use.

Velo looked carefully at his own kit. He did not intend to be caught in any carelessness or neglect of duty. He had cast aside as unsafe the idea of skipping away. It was more dangerous than the falling shells. He, like many another, had become calloused. On battlefields men move with as much of a sense of security as though they were invisible. It is not so much that they are not afraid as that they grow into a feeling that the dreadful din, the rattle and bang and dirt and blood, the anguish of men and horses, the distorted and ghastly deaths, will pass them by. The whine of bullets, and the spiteful snarl of exploding shells seems as much an incident as the tin rainfall and the wooden thunder on the stage.

Zaidos noticed this, and felt it himself. He saw men go singing along the trenches to their death, singing love songs and tender little ballads that had to do with flowers and larks and English lanes in May. And most of all he noticed that the face of every wounded man held a look of surprise in greater or less degree; of amazement, as though the outraged body said, "Has this thing come to *me*? Impossible!" The look was on the dead lying sprawled and twisted in the last silent paralysis of humanity. And although the dead and dying and wounded lay like warnings of a coming fate, although men tossed and reared grotesquely, and shattered horses screamed shrilly in throes of blind agony, the unhurt thousands moved on or lay in their trenches giving fire for fire, death for death without a quiver of concern.

Out into the worst of it went the boys together, Zaidos filled with the high courage of one who does his duty whole-heartedly, and is too busy with the task to wonder at his own fate, Velo with the unconcern of the panther who creeps sure-footedly along the crumbling ledge after his prey. With the noise, the sights and confusion of battle, a kind of madness grew in Velo. The words "To-day, to-day, to-day!" made a sort of song within him. He had all the time in the world. He liked to see Zaidos working, working, tiring himself out. It didn't really matter when he put Zaidos out. He only knew that sooner or later he would do it. He had become a criminal. The evil had wrecked his soul.

The boys worked with furious zeal. When the final toll of this dreadful war is taken, high up on the lists of fame, supreme in the immortal and shining roster of the saints, should stand the names of the men and women of the Red Cross. The zeal of fighting could not uphold them. The lust of battle could not inflame their courage. It was theirs to walk unguarded in the red rain of death, to kneel where the shells fell thickest, to pass through the line of deadly fire with their pitiful burdens.

Doing only good, bringing relief and rescue, they, too, have fallen, hundreds of them, victims of a struggle in which they had no active part.

Zaidos and that dark shadow, Velo, knelt beside a wounded soldier, and strove to save his life, while a black robed priest knelt beside the conscious man. He made the responses of his Church clearly and evenly. He listened while the chaplain commended him to the mercy of God. With an even voice he gave his name and sent a last passionately loving message to one he loved. Then while the boys still doggedly strove to stay his passing, he began to speak. His voice changed to the shrill, clear tones of childhood. He forgot the sonorous Latin of a moment past. He looked up and folded his hands.

"Mary, Mother, meek and mild,
Hear me, then a little child—"

He went on with the childish prayer. Velo stood up. Zaidos, kneeling, shook his head, waited until the voice trailed into silence, and folded his kit. They had come too late. The priest stood for a moment in prayer. The boys moved on, but Zaidos looked back. He was just in time to see the priest, with that strange look of wonder dawning on his face, sink slowly to his knees, and droop across the dead man's breast. A bullet was in his heart.

"I wish it would end," cried Zaidos passionately.

Velo smiled.

"Don't do that!" cried Zaidos wildly. "You are not half tending to your work. Get busy with this man here." He knelt beside a soldier as he spoke, and tried to change his position so he could tie up a gushing wound. Zaidos, who had done all the heavy work, was almost exhausted. His hands trembled a little. Time had rushed by, or else it had stood perfectly still since the first shot split the morning stillness. He had not eaten; he couldn't. On one of the trips with the heavy stretcher the doctor had given him something in a glass to take, but he had put it down for a moment, and Velo had spilled it. It had not seemed worth while to ask for more.

The battle roared around them. The enemy had pressed through the first wire entanglement, and a terrific hand-to-hand conflict was in progress. Then men charged with

James Fiske

bayonet on gun in the right hand, a short, keen knife in their teeth, and on their left hands a band set with spiked steel knuckles. They leaped into the trenches, struck once with the bayonet, let the musket go, and continued the fight with knife and knuckles. The boys seemed to be the center of a horrible whirlpool or eddy of fighting.

"Give me a bandage!" screamed Zaidos.

Velo, all unconscious of the battle about, stood looking down at Zaidos. His bloodshot eyes were narrowed to slits, his lips drawn back in a wolfish snarl. In his hand was a revolver. He leaned forward a little. He spoke, but in the din Zaidos could not hear his words. He could read the twisting lips, however.

"I've got the papers!" was what he said. He took careful, open aim with the revolver, and before Zaidos could move or spring, he fired straight at Zaidos' face!

Then he stood looking at the fallen boy. Zaidos lay on his back, arms spread wide, knees partly bent under him. Somehow he looked very young. Velo, once more conscious of the roar of guns, looked about him. The battle raged madly. As if drawn by a magnet, his gaze traveled back to the face of his victim. Sure enough, he had killed him. Zaidos was out of his way forever. He felt in his blouse where the precious papers were, then, moved by some strange impulse, he took them out, and held them up before the unseeing eyes of his cousin.

"All here; all here!" he said thickly. "Now *I'm* Zaidos; *I'm* head of the house!" Still holding the papers in his hand, he threw the revolver far from him. It had done its work. He nodded to Zaidos. "All here!" he repeated, fingering the pocket. "*I'm*—"

Something or someone seemed to strike him a violent blow in the back. It surprised him. He turned to see the offender. There was no one near. The tide of battle had swept past. He looked inquiringly at Zaidos, and idly dropped the papers on the ground, as he put a hand to his breast. Suddenly he lost interest in everything but the cause of the blow. He wondered what in the world had hit him. Not a bullet. Surely a bullet did not make you feel so numb and queer! He balanced back and forth as though he was walking a tight rope. Still staring at Zaidos, and still pressing a hand to his chest, he went slowly, very slowly, to his knees.

"That's strange," he said to Zaidos. Then without warning, he coughed. It tore, and ripped, and rent him with mortal agony. He screamed aloud. He clutched with both hands at his breast, screamed, and screamed and screamed, and so went slowly down and down, a million miles into blackness, and lay without further motion, his head against Zaidos' knee.

CHAPTER XI

DAYS OF WAITING

Inch by inch, step by step, yard after yard, the enemy forced the English back. They reached the second line of wire entanglements, where for awhile the battle raged, while Zaidos and Velo, like other thousands of silent and bloody figures, lay in strange, distorted groups.

At the second entanglement, however, something seemed to happen. Perhaps the enemy's charge had exhausted them, perhaps because a bulldog courage always fills the British. The tide turned. Once more the ground was covered. The first entanglement was reached and crossed. The havoc grew; the rout was turned into a victory. The Allies had won the day!

They followed the fleeing enemy, stubbornly hammering their rear as they retreated, while a thin sprinkle of Red Cross aids and doctors and nurses commenced to appear on that dreadful field. They moved here and there, clear stars in the dark sky of history.

One of them stopped to bandage a head where a clean line of blood showed a deep furrow in the side. When the wound was bandaged, the surgeon administered a dose of medicine, and in a moment Zaidos opened his eyes, and looked curiously up at the doctor.

"You are all right," said the doctor. "Nothing but a scratch on the head. Lie still and wig-wag the ambulance when it comes along."

He moved rapidly away, and Zaidos obeyed his parting order. In fact he was not able to move. Velo's bullet had cut close to the skull and Zaidos had lost much blood. He was conscious also of a pain in his broken leg, but could not move to see what caused it. Finally the aching grew so intense that it drove him to an upright position, although for a moment things whirled, and he was forced to close his eyes. When he looked he saw Velo, the anguish and pallor and amazement of death written on his face, lying doubled against Zaidos' knee. Carefully he worked himself free, to find that a bullet had struck his leg while he was unconscious, and had broken the small bone below the knee. It was the broken leg, at that. He straightened himself as well as he could, and looked at Velo. He commenced to remember. It came back bit by bit; the fight, and Velo's treachery. Last of all he remembered what Velo had said. "I have the papers!" So it was Velo all the time! Zaidos could not imagine how Velo had secured them. He knew when he had lost them that night in the barracks at Saloniki. Velo certainly had not been there. His hurt head beat painfully, and it was difficult for him to think. If Velo had the papers, however, he must get them. Velo was dead apparently. Zaidos knew that look. The papers were his. He must take them before someone came and carried him away. He knew what Velo's resting place would be, and shuddered. Slowly, painfully, he shifted his position until he lay close at his cousin's side. Supporting himself on his elbow, with his free hand he felt in the blood-stained blouse. The pockets were empty. Zaidos felt again. Then it seemed as though he could feel a faint heartbeat. It was so feeble that when Zaidos laid his hand on the torn breast and waited, he could feel no stir. He managed to get at his Aid kit, however, and drop by drop coaxed down a dose of strong restorative. He pressed a pad of gauze against the wound, and secured it with adhesive tape. He could see that the wound came through from the back, but he did not dare turn him over. Presently a faint sigh parted the lips, and Zaidos administered another dose.

Velo lived!

He opened his eyes presently, and looked dully at Zaidos. Then he recognized him, and a wild look crossed his face.

"Didn't I kill you?" he asked in a whisper.

"No," said Zaidos. There seemed to be nothing else to say.

"I tried to," said Velo.

"Don't talk!" said Zaidos. He didn't know what to say to the boy who had nearly taken his life in cold blood. It was murder. The slow deliberation of the thing chilled him. He had read of things like that; of innocent people who injured no one being killed in order that someone might unjustly enjoy something they possessed. He had been ready to stand by Velo and see that he was all right always. And Velo must have known it. No matter what he had said, Velo must have known that! Yet Velo had tried to kill him. He had seen the leveled revolver, and besides, Velo had just told him, as though he didn't in the least mind his knowing. As a matter of fact, Velo did care; but he was so near the shadowy borderland that lies between the living and the dead, that there was nothing left for him but the truth. And because of that, he continued, "I'm sorry, Zaidos."

But Zaidos would not reply.

"I'm sorry, Zaidos," Velo said again in his thick, queer whisper. "Will you forgive me?"

"No," said Zaidos suddenly. "No, I won't! What did I ever do to you that you should try to take my life? If I said I forgive you it would be a lie. Besides, you can't be sorry right off like that. As soon as you get well, you will try it again."

"Oh, I *am* sorry!" said Velo. "You *must* forgive me, Zaidos. I am too badly hurt to get well; you will not be troubled again. I know how I am wounded. So I am going to talk as much as I can. I wish you would take the papers. I stole them from you at the barracks. I got permission to go in while you were asleep. I thought you wouldn't be there, and I wanted to look for you and say that I couldn't find you, and so call the attention of the officers to your absence. The night your father died, you know. But you were there asleep, and I felt in your blouse, and found the packet. You had better get it out of my jacket now."

Zaidos unwillingly felt once more through the pocket. "It is empty," he said.

Velo thought a moment.

"I had it in my hand just now," he said. "Look on the ground."

The papers lay beside Velo's hand. Zaidos picked them up, and put them in his pocket.

"I have them," he said gruffly.

"I'm glad of that," said Velo. "Zaidos, I sold my soul for

those papers. I have been a bad boy all my life, not because I had bad surroundings, not because I was neglected. Your father was as good to me as he could be. I just thought it was smart to be bad. I don't think I hated you because of all your money and your title as much as I did because I knew you were square. I knew it as soon as you came into your father's house that night. I could see it in your face, and hear it in your voice, and feel it in your hand-shake. I knew you would never stand for the sort of life I led, and I hated you for it, Zaidos. And so it went from bad to worse, until I shot at you. You *must* forgive me, Zaidos!"

"I can't," said Zaidos stubbornly. "What's the use of my saying I do, if I don't?"

"Oh, you *must* forgive me!" begged the dying boy. "I am so sorry, so sorry! You can't see anyone as sorry as I am and not forgive them. Please, Zaidos! I can't bear it unless you do!"

"No," said Zaidos again.

Velo did not speak. When you are asked to forgive a wrong, and you refuse, it turns the punishment on you. Velo was silent, but Zaidos commenced to suffer. He could feel himself growing hard and cruel. After all, Velo had not succeeded in injuring him much, and Velo himself was dying fast. He could see it. But something kept him silent. He could not say the words Velo had begged to hear, and he stared back while Velo looked at him with dumb and suffering eyes.

"Oh, forgive me!" begged Velo with a dry sob that racked him. "Zaidos, be as good as you can, but don't be hard! You can't tell what temptations people have. It is a terrible thing to be hard. Don't do it, Zaidos! There are so many hard people—hard teachers and hard fathers who don't know how fellows are tempted and how they suffer. I am dying, Zaidos, and I tell you don't be hard. Forgive me!"

"I do!" said Zaidos quite suddenly. "I do, Velo! I mean it!"

Everything changed. He felt a kindliness and affection for Velo.

"You will get well, Velo, and we'll hit it off like twins."

"It's too late," said Velo, smiling; "too late for anything except to be happy to think you have forgiven me. Besides, it is as well for me to go. I think I'm a bad sort, Zaidos.... But I'm—so—glad—you—will—forgive me—"

There was a long silence. Then Velo opened his eyes once more.

"I'm going," he whispered. "Take my hand—"

Zaidos did so, and for a long, long time did not stir. The hand in his grew limp, then very cold. Zaidos held it loyally but he kept his eyes shut tight, because he could not bear to look.

The Red Cross orderlies did not find Zaidos until after dark. He was very cold, or else very hot, he did not know which, but tried to tell them all about it, and only succeeded in mumbling very fast before he dropped off into uncon- sciousness. He could not say farewell to Velo, lying there under the stars with a noble company about him. He was silent enough himself until he reached the big field hospital in the rear. He did not know Nurse Helen when she bent over him, but he commenced to talk in a low tone, and he kept on, as though he would never stop.

He told her all about everything, including a green dragon that sat on his leg, and felt heavy. He told her school jokes, and about the girl who came to the hop and about several million other things. Fever raged in him and his voice went down and down until it was as thin as a field mouse's squeak. Nurse Helen grew to look at him gravely and rather sadly and she spent no time at all with Tony Hazelden, who was almost well enough to get married. At least he could sit up an hour every day. But at last one day there came a change. Zaidos gave a sigh, and stopped talking and went to sleep.

The next time he opened his eyes, he looked straight into Nurse Helen's great, lovely, dark pools of silence and content. He looked at her a long time; then without speaking, he went to sleep again. The next time he woke up, he managed to whisper, "Got a lot to tell you!"

"Let it wait," she whispered back. "Don't talk at all. You will get well much sooner."

She was right, and he did, making great jumps toward recovery when he once got started. The time came when she let him talk and Zaidos told her all about everything. He even told her how hard he had been and how long it had taken him to forgive Velo.

So the days went on smoothly. Zaidos did not know how many; but one morning there awoke in him a great longing for his adopted land. And that happened to be the very morning when he heard something that might have made him very unhappy, but did not.

The doctor came along.

"What are you going to do with yourself when we discharge you, young man?" he demanded.

"I suppose I'll have to go back on the field," Zaidos replied.

"Don't you want to?" asked the doctor.

"I can't really say I do," said Zaidos regretfully. "You see I've never had the chance to fight. I was lame when they put me at the Hospital Corps work. At least my broken leg was tender. Now it's shot up, and I won't be good for anything else but Red Cross jobs."

"I may as well tell you," said the doctor. "You will always be a little lame, Zaidos. Not much, understand, but enough to bar you from any work here. I'm sorry, son. We did our best, but that shin bone didn't heal right. You have been given your 'honorable discharge."

For a little Zaidos was silent. No more running; no more jumping. It was a little hard, but he thought of the wounds of others, and was ashamed.

"Will I have to walk with a cane, doctor!" he asked.

"Oh, no," said the doctor. "Your limp will scarcely be noticeable."

"Then I guess I'll get on my job," said Zaidos, unconsciously quoting the boys at school.

"What's that?" asked the doctor.

"Why," said Zaidos, "I planned to go back to New York after all this was over, and study medicine."

"Couldn't do a better thing," said the doctor heartily. "That's the best thing you could possibly do. Nurse Helen has told me something about you, and I will say that I think you have planned wisely and well. If you had ties of family in this part of the world, it might be a different matter. No one has any right to carve out his destiny without some reference to the people nearest him. 'Honor thy father and thy mother' holds good to-day as well as it did when the old patriarchs walked the earth. And I'm not sure it isn't needed now more than it was then, when the scheme of life was simpler. Only now we usually have a few sisters and brothers, and perhaps an unmarried aunt or two to consider. But you are all alone, are you not?"

"Yes," said Zaidos. "I couldn't be more alone without being gone myself. I have lots of friends in school and I know a fellow in England; and so it's not so bad."

"No," said the doctor. "I should call it very good. And you have already found out, Zaidos, that sometimes blood relations fail a man.

"I think I will write out a discharge for you, and as soon as you can move you had better get away, and move toward the first seaport where you can get an American ship. I will pull all the wires I can. You had a pretty bad fever, my boy. You need a change, and you need it soon. I'll see what I can do. In the meantime, lie still and get your strength together. Things are frightfully crowded, but a lot of supplies and more nurses have been promised. Has Nurse Helen told you any news?"

"No," said Zaidos, "not a thing. About the hospital, do you mean, doctor?"

"Not exactly," said the doctor, smiling. "Just some little plans of her own."

"I'll bet Tony Hazelden is in them!" said Zaidos.

The doctor chuckled. "Well, these girls! You never can tell," he said. "She will tell you herself, I've no doubt."

He got up and straightened his bent back. "This sort of thing is hard on an old man," he said. "It is just two weeks since I have been to bed."

"Well, this one feels good to me," said Zaidos. "I was so surprised when I woke up and found something smooth and clean under me. I don't see how the nurses manage to keep things so neat."

"You would not wonder if you could see what they do," said the doctor solemnly. "I tell you every woman who goes into the field deserves a place in the Legion of Honor. She deserves a crown, and a big pension. She's an angel. You want to honor all women, all kinds, all your life, my boy, for the sake of these nurses. Some day, perhaps, I will come over to your America, if you would like to see an old derelict, and we will talk and talk, and I will tell you some stories."

He touched Zaidos' bandaged head gently, nodded farewell and walked on down the line of cots. Zaidos continued to sleep and eat. His blood was so clean that his wounds healed almost at once. Helen came to his bedside one day with a queer little smile on her face.

"Do you remember, John, what I said when you brought Tony to me? I told you that just as soon as he was able to hold my hand, I meant to marry him."

"Did you do it?" asked Zaidos.

"Not yet," said Helen.

"Goodness!" said Zaidos. "I didn't think Tony was as sick as all that! I would have to be a good deal worse than he looks to be so sick I couldn't hold your hand!"

"Silly!" said Helen, blushing. "If you will attend with the gravity the occasion requires, I will explain things to you. Perhaps Tony has been able to hold my hand a *little*; but he was not strong enough to hold it very hard. Now, however, he is growing better fast. On the other hand, the doctors say *I* am worn out. I don't think so myself. I think they are making it up, the dears, so I can honorably go home with Tony. But be that as it may, I am going home. We are going to be married a week from tomorrow, John, dear, and then in a few days I will begin to move my dear Tony by slow stages homeward. And I want you to come with us."

"Me on a honeymoon trip? Well, I think not!" Zaidos exploded. "Nay, nay, pretty lady, you won't get me to chaperone you!"

"Now, John!" cried Helen. "Oh, I could shake you! What will I do crossing Europe with a sick man on a cot, unless someone comes to help me? I didn't think you were so ungallant!"

Zaidos stared at her. "That's another way to look at it," he said. "Of course I will go with you, and glad enough to do it. I never thought of that, Helen. Of course you could not go alone! Why can't I get up and go talk things over with Tony? You can't yell that sort of conversation the whole length of a ward."

"You are to be allowed to get up tomorrow," said Helen, "and, oh, John, *please* get well fast, because really I don't see how we can go without you. No one else can be spared, and I want to go home. I want to see my father and mother. Just think of it, I will have to be married all alone. Not one of my own people to give me away, and kiss me, and say, 'God bless you.' I suppose I am an ungrateful girl. I ought to be thinking only that I have Tony, and how happy I am; but you know after all, John, a girl's wedding day is a wonderful time. It is all so different to what we had planned. At home, we would have had the service in our own dear church, trimmed by all the little girls in the parish. And everyone would be there. The church would not hold them; the churchyard would be full of beaming faces, everybody bobbing and curtsying and wishing us good luck. And if I felt that I *must* shed a few happy tears, my mother's shoulder would be near."

"Do you *have* to cry?" asked Zaidos.

"Why, I don't suppose one *has* to," said Helen musingly, "but generally you do."

"That's awful," said Zaidos dismally, and then repeated, "Awful! However, I don't know the first thing about girls, and of course you do. If you must cry on somebody, why, you must; and you can use me, if you like."

CHAPTER XII

GREATER THINGS

A week flew past. In the convalescent ward there was the greatest amount of suppressed excitement. All the soldiers loved Helen, and they showered her with queer, pathetic little gifts, always the best of their poor store of belongings. Tony was not to leave his cot. He would have to be moved across Europe on a stretcher, but he lay beaming at the men who called good wishes to him in half a dozen languages.

The wedding morning dawned clear and beautiful. Every soldier who could hobble was out early gathering flowers and boughs with which they trimmed the ward. Helen, who was a hundred yards away, in the nurses' tent, knew nothing of all this. An hour before she was to come to meet Tony, the old doctor, bearing a large package, stood before the tent.

"My dear," he said awkwardly when Helen appeared, "I—er—wanted to do something for you, and it gave me a good deal of happiness to pretend that you were my own daughter, if you don't object. I happen to have a sister in Paris, and I telegraphed her a week ago. I think I have heard you say you were size thirty-six. Well, my dear, this package has just come. She sent it in care of a reserve of nurses. You see—ha—hum—the men will be so pleased. Now you put it on if it is fit for you, and wear it, with the love of a grateful old man." He turned and abruptly walked away as Helen untied the box, but he could not so escape from those swift feet. There was a cry as the girl peered beneath the papers, and then a swift rush toward him. So it happened that it was not Zaidos' reluctant and unaccustomed shoulder on which the happy tears were shed, and it was not to Tony that Helen's last tender girl-kisses were given.

And when the time came for the simple, sad little ceremony in the hospital ward, it was not a dark clad nurse who walked between the cots on the doctor's arm, but such a vision of loveliness that the men gasped and Tony turned so pale that the aid beside him reached for the spirits of ammonia. For the doctor's present was a wedding dress, just as satiny and lacy and long as any bride in Mayfair could have worn.

The veil covered her lovely face, and through it her dark eyes lingered tenderly on the eager white faces that lined her path. And last they rested on Tony. Zaidos caught the look, and it made him feel that he would do most anything to have anyone look at him like that. It was a look that a fellow could never bear unless he had lived a clean and honest life. Zaidos, seeing this wonderful look that was meant for Tony alone, glanced quickly away and somehow it was he, down in his innermost heart, who longed for a shoulder to cry on!

In a few short minutes the little ceremony was over, and a musical genius played the wedding march on a mouth-organ so you'd know it anywhere. He followed that with *God Save the King*, and *Tipperary*, while Helen, looking more like an angel every minute, walked slowly down the aisle, shaking hands with the men. She came at last to one whose arms were both gone. Without a moment's hesitation she stooped and pressed a kiss on the upturned brow. Another moment with a last smile and wave of her hand, she was gone,

James Fiske

leaving the men with their beautiful memory.

Zaidos asked the doctor, who was openly wiping his eyes, to speak with him a moment outside.

"You know my cousin is out there," he said, with a wave of the arm at the field where great trenches made a resting place for hundreds of unknown men. "I've been trying to think of something to do for him, something to remember him by. I couldn't think of anything. First I thought of a monument; and then I thought of tablets in the church at Saloniki. Then it just happened to come to me, that why not do something for our field hospital here. When I get to England I will arrange to have the money sent you. Do you approve of that?"

"Of course I do, my boy," said the doctor heartily. "Of course I approve! Any help would be most gratefully accepted. You know how short we are for everything. Send anything you feel like affording. Any little sum you happen to want to give."

"I was wondering about five hundred dollars a month, while the war lasts," said Zaidos musingly. "Would that make much difference?"

"Five—five hundred American dollars?" screamed the doctor. "*A hundred pounds*? You don't mean that, do you? Why, hum—haw—can you afford it?"

"Oh, yes," said Zaidos simply. "I suppose I can afford almost anything I want. I had a long talk with my father the night he died, so I happen to know just what my income is. And I don't spend much. There isn't anything to spend it for. Of course, when I go back to school, I mean to put up a new gymnasium. The one we have is a freak; but that won't break me, either."

"A hundred pounds!" said the doctor. Delightful visions of endless rolls of bandages, antiseptics, medicines, nurses, litters, shelter tents, beds, and food appeared before the doctor's delighted eyes. "A hundred pounds!" he repeated. "Zaidos, Zaidos, you will erect a monument to your cousin finer—" he choked, then turned, and with an arm over Zaidos' shoulder continued: "Well, Zaidos, it is hard for an Englishman, and an old Englishman at that, to express what he feels; but, my boy, I am as proud of you as though you were my own son! Proud of you, Zaidos! You are perfectly sure you mean it?"

"Of course," said Zaidos, laughing. "I think the thing to do is to put money in a bank and fix it so you yourself can draw it, as needed, at the rate of five hundred a month. I'll be busy in school catching up so I won't be able to see to it."

"Wonderful! Wonderful!" said the doctor. "I think I will go see the General, Zaidos. I have got to tell someone. I can never keep all this to myself."

He went hurrying off and Zaidos watched him. Once he bumped into a tree and twice an orderly called him. He made no reply. He was thinking with whirling brain of the lives he would be able to save.

Then he reached the General's tent, and burst in unceremoniously. They had been classmates at college.

"Dick," cried the doctor, "Dick, the most amazing thing has happened!" and with a rush of words he poured out the fine news.

"Well, bless me, bless me!" cried the General, shoving back

from the table where a map of Europe was spread. "Now, Henry, I know just how well pleased you are. Why, what wonderful things you can do with all that money! But are you sure the lad will do as he says?"

"You ought to know that lad, Dick!" exploded the doctor. "He's the finest boy! He's just what you would have wanted your boy to be like, if you had loved some girl, and had married her, and had had a baby, and it had grown up. He won't disappoint me, rest assured of that!"

And Zaidos didn't.

When, after a long, slow and anxious journey, Helen and Tony and Zaidos finally reached London, Zaidos left the young married pair in the charge of a full battalion of relatives that had advanced in close formation as their train drew into the station, and proceeded at once to the office of a lawyer who was none other than Tony's cousin Jack. It took only a couple of days to fix the thing all up for the doctor; indeed, it was so tied up with red tape and all that, that Zaidos was not sure anyone would *ever* get the money.

Jack was more than nice to Zaidos, and insisted on taking him to his own quarters, where he rested quietly for several days. The journey had been harder than Zaidos had realized. His leg ached, and it was slow work getting around on crutches. As soon as Jack could get away, he suggested that they should go down to Hazelden, and see for themselves if Tony was improving as much as the family claimed.

They went on the train, for Jack had given up his motor car as his donation to the war fund. In the station, as Zaidos was hobbling painfully along, a husky youth in uniform bumped into him, and nearly knocked him over. He apologized.

"All right, Nick, all right!" said Zaidos joyously.

The husky youth stared, then gave a very un-English whoop, and made a bear rush at Zaidos. When he had finished patting him on the back and stuttering all sorts of inquiries, he managed to make a few questions clear. Where was he going? What for? Who was he going to stay with? When was he coming back? If it wasn't rotten, *rotten* luck that he was just off for Paris on government business!

When Zaidos could get a word in edgewise, he broke it to Nickell-Wheelerson that he was going away from England, back to America—and to that end his passage was already secured on a vessel leaving in a week's time. He was going down to visit some people named Hazelden.

"My second cousins, by Jove!" averred Nick, delighted. "A week? Well, if I can smooth things over between the Allies and Germany, in less than that time, I'll come down and ask them to put me up for a day." He patted Zaidos again. "It certainly seems good to see you, old chap! Here's my train, so I must go. Don't forget me, and I'll get down before you leave, if I can."

He dashed for the door the porter held open for him, and with a last wave of the hand was carried out of sight. When Jack returned, Zaidos told him about the encounter, and Jack laughed.

"Of course he's a cousin," he said. "One of the nicest fellows I know. Didn't know you knew him. Odd about its being such a little world and all that, don't you think?" He laughed. "Once I met a chap in India way up in the mountains. I was running around a bit, and he was tracking down a lost tribe or something of the sort. A while after that I walked into dad's billiard room at home, and there was the Johnny playing billiards with himself, cool as you please! He stopped, and said, 'Hullo, didn't know you knew I this family!'

"I said, 'Didn't know you knew them, either.'

"'Relations, perhaps?' he asked.

"'Yes, parents,' I told him, and then we had a jolly gas."

Jack waited on Zaidos with such care all the way down from London that the boy said he would be entirely spoiled. A big, roomy car met them at the station and carried them smoothly over miles of perfect road through the vast park of the Hazelden's where pheasants by the dozen flew across their path, bright-eyed deer dashed into hiding, and hundreds of wonderful Persian sheep grazed on the lawns that had been lawns for generations.

It seemed strange to see Helen in filmy summer dress instead of the severe uniform of a nurse, and Zaidos missed the white cap on her beautiful hair, but he decided finally that she was even prettier without it. Zaidos could not keep from watching her every move. She ordered Tony about with a pretty air of sternness, but with such a look of loving devotion that it was easy to see the reason for the young man's look of contentment.

The days flew past as though on wings. Helen's younger sister proved to be a second edition of Helen, even prettier if possible, and Zaidos found himself wondering how he could ever have given a thought to the blonde damsel whom he had met at the hop so long ago. Before it came time to go, Zaidos caught himself regarding Helen in a new light. He found himself thinking that she would be a very pleasant person to have in the family! And that was going a long, long way for Zaidos!

He had news for Helen. A letter from the old doctor, with pages of thanks and plans for the use of the money. Of course Helen had to hear it all, and afternoons they would all sit on the terrace together, and talk of the future and make pleasant plans.

Of the past, of the dreadful days on the stained battlefields of the Dardanelles, they spoke little. Some day perhaps when time had mellowed the colors, then this group of young people could talk it over. Just now the price they had paid for their experiences seemed too great. It was all too near. They tried to put it behind them, as all the world will have to do when at last this war is over, when the last gun calls its death challenge, when all the submarines rise to the surface of the outraged sea, and the last war Zeppelin settles to earth. On that day, a curtain must fall over this terrible middle-act in modern history, to rise again on new and nobler things.

The group on the terrace, enjoying the warm afternoon sun, often kept the mournful silence of those who have known all war's horrors, yet they were filled with deepest thankfulness that they were spared to each other.

The old Earl followed Tony in his invalid chair with adoring eyes. Every day, a dozen women, ladies of high degree, assembled and sewed or knit for the soldiers. The great county houses on either side were given over as convalescent homes. Fairs, bazaars, teas, meetings filled the days. England gave all her time and strength for the soldiers.

When Zaidos found a chance to read the doctor's letter to Helen she was so pleased with it that she insisted on taking it and reading it to a number of the committees that seemed to be meeting from morning until night. The letter gave a clear view of the needs of the Red Cross, and told so well of the good it was doing. And to his horror, Zaidos was invited to address three separate organizations. Helen refused for him after he had threatened to run away by night and walk to London.

Nick evidently had trouble with the Allies or the Germans, because he did not come down, and sent no word.

It came time for Zaidos to leave. The last night he was there he wrote a bunch of letters. The first was addressed to school, and commenced:

Fellows:

Well, after all, I'm coming back. Such a lot of things have happened that there is no use writing about them at all. I'll tell you all that it's good for you to hear when I see you. Only there's no reason for me to stay here now as there is now no one in this country belonging to me. My only relative, a cousin about my age, was shot and killed. And I got nipped a little. So they don't want me any more, and I'm coming back on the next steamer. If you can get it, I want my old room.

I'm visiting some fine people here in the country. Met 'em on the battlefield. At least I met two of them there. I saw Nick in London, but he's in France now. You know he's an Earl; but it doesn't seem to worry him. He stepped all over me just the same as ever, and was just as sorry. He wears a uniform, of course, so I don't know if his neckties are as bad as ever they used to be.

It's going to be good to see you. I guess after all I have told you all the news. Nothing much has happened, as you see.

There's a girl here; you never saw anything like her. Say, she makes me feel sorry for you way off there!

Well, so long, boys! I'll see you soon, if we don't get torpedoed. They don't make many plans over here. They say, "Do come and see me to-morrow if you don't get Zeppelined." So long!

ZAIDOS.

Zaidos folded this letter with the pleased consciousness that he had written a lot of news.

The next was for the doctor.

"Dear Doctor," he wrote, "I'm at the Hazeldens; and they are about the nicest people in the world. Among other members of the family, Mrs. Hazelden, who was Miss Helen, has a sister who seems a pleasant young lady. I will soon leave for America; and except for leaving the Hazeldens, as well as Helen's sister, who seems real pleasant, I shall be glad to go. I do hate to hang around and do nothing. A million people come here every day and work for the soldiers. I think the men would appreciate it if they could know the amount of tea it takes to keep them going here while they sew.

The money is all fixed up. I do hope you will enjoy spending it. Let me hear from you some day, doctor. Perhaps that is asking a good deal, but it would be fine if you could spare time.

I often think of Velo. Somehow he seems different to me now. There were a lot of things about Velo that used to make me mad, but which now I do not seem to remember. It is a great pity that he died. Perhaps if he had lived, and I had taken him back to school with me, he would have had a different life. I don't know. Anyway, somehow I think of him a good deal, and I'm glad I do, because it must be awful to have no one at all to think of you after you are dead.

I will write again when I get back to America, doctor. Don't forget me and don't forget that I am going to try to be as great a surgeon as you are.

Your friend,
ZAIDOS."

The third letter was written in modern Greek, using the familiar "thee" and "thou" of intimate speech.

My old Nurse Maratha:

The war kept me from thee, when at last I could get away. I would have come to Saloniki if I could but I had an errand that took me straight to England.

Velo is dead, Maratha. He was shot in the big battle. You must have been praying when he died, if I know thee still. And I was shot, too, a little, and must ever walk lame. I tell thee this so no one else may tell thee first. I am only a *little* lame, though. In a day or two I take ship for America and so back to school, as thou heardst His Highness, my father, plan that last night. Close the house, and go thou to the lodge. Keep all the servants who have served my father for more than ten years and pay them from the money I shall send thee each month. And be very good to Maratha, for I shall come back some day, and she must not be too old or too lame to take care of me.

Good-bye, Maratha.
I am always Thy boy,
ZAIDOS.

Zaidos sealed the letters and sent them off with a sigh of relief. He had now but one cause of worry. He had promised to write to Helen's sister, and he didn't know what to say! He forgot the fact that he would not have to write the letter until he reached America. But at last he forgot even that when the parting came.

Helen tore herself away from Tony and went down to London to see him off; and Jack went rushing around making all sorts of work for himself. They were early at the pier, and, after Zaidos' baggage was settled in his stateroom, the three people sauntered back to the dock for the half hour that remained before the first warning call. Three familiar figures came down, looking here and there. Helen saw them and exclaimed, "Why, there's father, and mother, and Alice!"

And sure as fate it was! The rector had had to take the next train for London most unexpectedly, and so thought he would bring his wife and daughter to join in the leave-takings.

So Zaidos had quite a little group of people waving him good-bye as the ship went slowly out into the west. But the gaze that held him longest and the face he saw the last was not Helen's!

Choose from Thousands of 1stWorldLibrary Classics By

A. M. Barnard	Booth Tarkington	Edward Everett Hale
Ada Leverson	Boyd Cable	Edward J. O'Biren
Adolphus William Ward	Bram Stoker	Edward S. Ellis
Aesop	C. Collodi	Edwin L. Arnold
Agatha Christie	C. E. Orr	Eleanor Atkins
Alexander Aaronsohn	C. M. Ingleby	Eleanor Hallowell Abbott
Alexander Kielland	Carolyn Wells	Eliot Gregory
Alexandre Dumas	Catherine Parr Traill	Elizabeth Gaskell
Alfred Gatty	Charles A. Eastman	Elizabeth McCracken
Alfred Ollivant	Charles Amory Beach	Elizabeth Von Arnim
Alice Duer Miller	Charles Dickens	Ellem Key
Alice Turner Curtis	Charles Dudley Warner	Emerson Hough
Alice Dunbar	Charles Farrar Browne	Emilie F. Carlen
Allen Chapman	Charles Ives	Emily Bronte
Alleyne Ireland	Charles Kingsley	Emily Dickinson
Ambrose Bierce	Charles Klein	Enid Bagnold
Amelia E. Barr	Charles Hanson Towne	Enilor Macartney Lane
Amory H. Bradford	Charles Lathrop Pack	Erasmus W. Jones
Andrew Lang	Charles Romyn Dake	Ernie Howard Pie
Andrew McFarland Davis	Charles Whibley	Ethel May Dell
Andy Adams	Charles Willing Beale	Ethel Turner
Angela Brazil	Charlotte M. Braeme	Ethel Watts Mumford
Anna Alice Chapin	Charlotte M. Yonge	Eugene Sue
Anna Sewell	Charlotte Perkins Stetson	Eugenie Foa
Annie Besant	Clair W. Hayes	Eugene Wood
Annie Hamilton Donnell	Clarence Day Jr.	Eustace Hale Ball
Annie Payson Call	Clarence E. Mulford	Evelyn Everett-green
Annie Roe Carr	Clemence Housman	Everard Cotes
Annonaymous	Confucius	F. H. Cheley
Anton Chekhov	Coningsby Dawson	F. J. Cross
Archibald Lee Fletcher	Cornelis DeWitt Wilcox	F. Marion Crawford
Arnold Bennett	Cyril Burleigh	Fannie E. Newberry
Arthur C. Benson	D. H. Lawrence	Federick Austin Ogg
Arthur Conan Doyle	Daniel Defoe	Ferdinand Ossendowski
Arthur M. Winfield	David Garnett	Fergus Hume
Arthur Ransome	Dinah Craik	Florence A. Kilpatrick
Arthur Schnitzler	Don Carlos Janes	Fremont B. Deering
Arthur Train	Donald Keyhoe	Francis Bacon
Atticus	Dorothy Kilner	Francis Darwin
B.H. Baden-Powell	Dougan Clark	Frances Hodgson Burnett
B. M. Bower	Douglas Fairbanks	Frances Parkinson Keyes
B. C. Chatterjee	E. Nesbit	Frank Gee Patchin
Baroness Emmuska Orczy	E. P. Roe	Frank Harris
Baroness Orczy	E. Phillips Oppenheim	Frank Jewett Mather
Basil King	E. S. Brooks	Frank L. Packard
Bayard Taylor	Earl Barnes	Frank V. Webster
Ben Macomber	Edgar Rice Burroughs	Frederic Stewart Isham
Bertha Muzzy Bower	Edith Van Dyne	Frederick Trevor Hill
Bjornstjerne Bjornson	Edith Wharton	Frederick Winslow Taylor

Friedrich Kerst
Friedrich Nietzsche
Fyodor Dostoyevsky
G.A. Henty
G.K. Chesterton
Gabrielle E. Jackson
Garrett P. Serviss
Gaston Leroux
George A. Warren
George Ade
Geroge Bernard Shaw
George Cary Eggleston
George Durston
George Ebers
George Eliot
George Gissing
George MacDonald
George Meredith
George Orwell
George Sylvester Viereck
George Tucker
George W. Cable
George Wharton James
Gertrude Atherton
Gordon Casserly
Grace E. King
Grace Gallatin
Grace Greenwood
Grant Allen
Guillermo A. Sherwell
Gulielma Zollinger
Gustav Flaubert
H. A. Cody
H. B. Irving
H. C. Bailey
H. G. Wells
H. H. Munro
H. Irving Hancock
H. R. Naylor
H. Rider Haggard
H. W. C. Davis
Haldeman Julius
Hall Caine
Hamilton Wright Mabie
Hans Christian Andersen
Harold Avery
Harold McGrath
Harriet Beecher Stowe
Harry Castlemon
Harry Coghill
Harry Houidini

Hayden Carruth
Helent Hunt Jackson
Helen Nicolay
Hendrik Conscience
Hendy David Thoreau
Henri Barbusse
Henrik Ibsen
Henry Adams
Henry Ford
Henry Frost
Henry James
Henry Jones Ford
Henry Seton Merriman
Henry W Longfellow
Herbert A. Giles
Herbert Carter
Herbert N. Casson
Herman Hesse
Hildegard G. Frey
Homer
Honore De Balzac
Horace B. Day
Horace Walpole
Horatio Alger Jr.
Howard Pyle
Howard R. Garis
Hugh Lofting
Hugh Walpole
Humphry Ward
Ian Maclaren
Inez Haynes Gillmore
Irving Bacheller
Isabel Cecilia Williams
Isabel Hornibrook
Israel Abrahams
Ivan Turgenev
J. G.Austin
J. Henri Fabre
J. M. Barrie
J. M. Walsh
J. Macdonald Oxley
J. R. Miller
J. S. Fletcher
J. S. Knowles
J. Storer Clouston
J. W. Duffield
Jack London
Jacob Abbott
James Allen
James Andrews
James Baldwin

James Branch Cabell
James DeMille
James Joyce
James Lane Allen
James Lane Allen
James Oliver Curwood
James Oppenheim
James Otis
James R. Driscoll
Jane Abbott
Jane Austen
Jane L. Stewart
Janet Aldridge
Jens Peter Jacobsen
Jerome K. Jerome
Jessie Graham Flower
John Buchan
John Burroughs
John Cournos
John F. Kennedy
John Gay
John Glasworthy
John Habberton
John Joy Bell
John Kendrick Bangs
John Milton
John Philip Sousa
John Taintor Foote
Jonas Lauritz Idemil Lie
Jonathan Swift
Joseph A. Altsheler
Joseph Carey
Joseph Conrad
Joseph E. Badger Jr
Joseph Hergesheimer
Joseph Jacobs
Jules Vernes
Julian Hawthrone
Julie A Lippmann
Justin Huntly McCarthy
Kakuzo Okakura
Karle Wilson Baker
Kate Chopin
Kenneth Grahame
Kenneth McGaffey
Kate Langley Bosher
Kate Langley Bosher
Katherine Cecil Thurston
Katherine Stokes
L. A. Abbot
L. T. Meade

L. Frank Baum
Latta Griswold
Laura Dent Crane
Laura Lee Hope
Laurence Housman
Lawrence Beasley
Leo Tolstoy
Leonid Andreyev
Lewis Carroll
Lewis Sperry Chafer
Lilian Bell
Lloyd Osbourne
Louis Hughes
Louis Joseph Vance
Louis Tracy
Louisa May Alcott
Lucy Fitch Perkins
Lucy Maud Montgomery
Luther Benson
Lydia Miller Middleton
Lyndon Orr
M. Corvus
M. H. Adams
Margaret E. Sangster
Margret Howth
Margaret Vandercook
Margaret W. Hungerford
Margret Penrose
Maria Edgeworth
Maria Thompson Daviess
Mariano Azuela
Marion Polk Angellotti
Mark Overton
Mark Twain
Mary Austin
Mary Catherine Crowley
Mary Cole
Mary Hastings Bradley
Mary Roberts Rinehart
Mary Rowlandson
M. Wollstonecraft Shelley
Maud Lindsay
Max Beerbohm
Myra Kelly
Nathaniel Hawthrone
Nicolo Machiavelli
O. F. Walton
Oscar Wilde
Owen Johnson
P.G. Wodehouse
Paul and Mabel Thorne

Paul G. Tomlinson
Paul Severing
Percy Brebner
Percy Keese Fitzhugh
Peter B. Kyne
Plato
Quincy Allen
R. Derby Holmes
R. L. Stevenson
R. S. Ball
Rabindranath Tagore
Rahul Alvares
Ralph Bonehill
Ralph Henry Barbour
Ralph Victor
Ralph Waldo Emmerson
Rene Descartes
Ray Cummings
Rex Beach
Rex E. Beach
Richard Harding Davis
Richard Jefferies
Richard Le Gallienne
Robert Barr
Robert Frost
Robert Gordon Anderson
Robert L. Drake
Robert Lansing
Robert Lynd
Robert Michael Ballantyne
Robert W. Chambers
Rosa Nouchette Carey
Rudyard Kipling
Saint Augustine
Samuel B. Allison
Samuel Hopkins Adams
Sarah Bernhardt
Sarah C. Hallowell
Selma Lagerlof
Sherwood Anderson
Sigmund Freud
Standish O'Grady
Stanley Weyman
Stella Benson
Stella M. Francis
Stephen Crane
Stewart Edward White
Stijn Streuvels
Swami Abhedananda
Swami Parmananda
T. S. Ackland

T. S. Arthur
The Princess Der Ling
Thomas A. Janvier
Thomas A Kempis
Thomas Anderton
Thomas Bailey Aldrich
Thomas Bulfinch
Thomas De Quincey
Thomas Dixon
Thomas H. Huxley
Thomas Hardy
Thomas More
Thornton W. Burgess
U. S. Grant
Upton Sinclair
Valentine Williams
Various Authors
Vaughan Kester
Victor Appleton
Victor G. Durham
Victoria Cross
Virginia Woolf
Wadsworth Camp
Walter Camp
Walter Scott
Washington Irving
Wilbur Lawton
Wilkie Collins
Willa Cather
Willard F. Baker
William Dean Howells
William le Queux
W. Makepeace Thackeray
William W. Walter
William Shakespeare
Winston Churchill
Yei Theodora Ozaki
Yogi Ramacharaka
Young E. Allison
Zane Grey

.

www.ingramcontent.com/pod-product-compliance
Lightning Source LLC
Chambersburg PA
CBHW051837170626
46807CB00003B/1232